Her door w[...]

Colt peeked over his shoulder, grateful nobody was around. But when it came time to actually put his fingers on the door handle, he hesitated.

And then his dog must've caught his scent from the room down the hall and began to bark.

"Mac!" he called out as softly as he could, immediately quieting the shepherd.

Colt opened Amber's door and slid inside before he could change his mind. If someone had heard his dog and came out to investigate, they'd see him standing there. Not good.

Forcing himself to open his eyes, he scanned her room. Bed to his left. Table and chairs to his right. There was a purse sitting on top of one of the chairs, wide open.

Go.

But he couldn't. He wasn't cut out for this. The idea of rummaging through her things… He just couldn't do it. He swung around to leave.

And came face-to-face with Amber.

Dear Reader,

It seems hard to believe this is my eighth Harlequin American Romance novel. It seems like yesterday that I made the decision to write about cowboys and the women they love, but I'll admit, I almost stopped writing them. As many of you know, my life has been chaotic with the recent loss of my parents. Something had to give and I decided my adult horse stories (as I call them) would be it. I can't tell you how many times I regretted that decision. So when my editor called and asked if I'd be interested in writing one more cowboy story, I jumped at the chance. Not only that, but I asked if I could write two.

It's good to be back!

I love each and every one of my books, but *Rancher and Protector* has a special place in my heart. The book is about horses and the power they have over special-needs children. I first heard about this magical bond when asked to review a book for a nationally known horse magazine. The story was about an autistic child who traveled to Mongolia to ride horses. Why? You'll have to read the story, but it was truly the inspiration for this book.

I hope you enjoy *Rancher and Protector*. As always, I enjoy hearing from readers. You can reach me on Facebook at www.facebook.com/pamelabritton or through my website www.pamelabritton.com.

Best,

Pamela

Rancher and Protector

PAMELA BRITTON

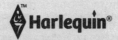

TORONTO NEW YORK LONDON
AMSTERDAM PARIS SYDNEY HAMBURG
STOCKHOLM ATHENS TOKYO MILAN MADRID
PRAGUE WARSAW BUDAPEST AUCKLAND

Recycling programs
for this product may
not exist in your area.

ISBN-13: 978-0-373-75377-2

RANCHER AND PROTECTOR

Copyright © 2011 by Pamela Britton

This edition published by arrangement with Harlequin Books S.A.

For questions and comments about the quality of this book please contact us at Customer_eCare@Harlequin.ca

www.Harlequin.com

Printed in U.S.A.

ABOUT THE AUTHOR

With over a million books in print, Pamela Britton likes to call herself the best known author nobody's ever heard of. Of course, that changed thanks to a certain licensing agreement with that little racing organization known as NASCAR.

But before the glitz and glamour of NASCAR, Pamela wrote books that were frequently voted the best of the best by *The Detroit Free Press,* Barnes & Noble (two years in a row) and *RT Book Reviews.* She's won numerous awards, including the National Reader's Choice Award and a nomination for the Romance Writers of America's Golden Heart.

When not writing books, Pamela is a reporter for a local newspaper. She's also a columnist for the *American Quarter Horse Journal. Rancher and Protector* is the author's twenty-sixth title.

Books by Pamela Britton

HARLEQUIN AMERICAN ROMANCE
  985—COWBOY LESSONS
1040—COWBOY TROUBLE
1122—COWBOY M.D.
1143—COWBOY VET
1166—COWGIRL'S CEO
1285—THE WRANGLER
1322—MARK, SECRET COWBOY

HQN BOOKS
DANGEROUS CURVES
IN THE GROOVE
ON THE EDGE
TO THE LIMIT
TOTAL CONTROL
ON THE MOVE

To the lawman who saved our homestead. Chris Ashworth, we couldn't have done it without you. All the words in this book couldn't express how grateful we are.

Chapter One

"All right, horse. We can do this the hard way or the easy way."

Amber Brooks stared at the animal in question, a tiny window placed high in the wall giving her a perfect view of the brown horse as it cocked its head in her direction. The look it gave her clearly indicated disdain.

"Okay, the hard way." Her hands tightened around the nylon strap someone had told her was a halter—although she had no idea how it worked.

"Just go play with a horse," she murmured under her breath, mimicking the camp director. "You'll do fine."

As if handling an animal as big as a bookcase would be "easy." What if it bolted out of the stall? Or charged in her direction? Or, God forbid, tried to bite her?

"Nice horsey horsey," she said. The animal's black mane seemed more of a dark gray in the stall's ambient light—like the color of a snake. She shivered.

Her feet felt heavy in the thick bed of pine shavings. "I'm not going to hurt you."

She stopped by its head and looked down at the halter. Now what? Obviously, the smaller hole went around the horse's nose. Or maybe its ear? But there was only one hole and so that didn't make sense. Nose, she decided.

A soft breath wafted across her crotch.

"Whoa," she cried, jumping back. "We don't know each other well enough for you to be doing that."

Someone coughed.

Amber turned in surprise to see John Wayne standing outside the stall.

Well, okay, it wasn't really John Wayne, but it sure was a cowboy. Black hat. Checkered beige shirt. *Cool blue eyes.*

"He's just trying to get to know you," the man said, his deep baritone splashed with a Southern accent. "He doesn't mean anything by it."

Easy for the cowboy to say. Amber couldn't take her eyes off her unexpected visitor. He was *gorgeous.* A hunk-o-hunk of burning love, as her friend Rachel would say. And just what was it about cowboys? They all looked the same. Five o'clock shadows. Square jaws. The smell of outdoors clinging to them. Was it part of the cowboy genome?

"I don't mean to be rude," she said. "But do I know you?"

He shook his head. "Colton Sheridan. I was hired on Thursday."

Just as she'd been, Amber thought. Well, she didn't get hired on Thursday, but she was new to Camp Cowboy, too.

"Gil sent me in here to help you out," he said.

Gil. The camp director. Gil and Buck had been looking for some additional help since the moment they'd realized their enrollment numbers were nearly triple what they'd been the previous year. Buck was off buying more horses, which left Gil in charge. Not many horses in the heart of San Francisco, but that's where the camp was. Amber once again marveled at their location—smack-dab in the middle of Golden Gate National Recreation Area. Step outside the barn and the high-rises were clearly visible in the distance.

"Nice to meet you, Colton, but I'd rather tackle this on my own."

That's what she was supposed to be doing: learning about horses. She'd come to Camp Cowboy committed to the idea of becoming a hippotherapist. Therapy was her thing. She specialized in speech therapy now, but she'd heard of some remarkable breakthroughs when children were exposed to horses. She might not like the animals, but she would get over that.

Anything for Dee.

She turned back to the horse. Its name was Flash, or so she'd read outside the stall. She hoped that didn't mean it'd trample her in a flash.

"It goes the other way," he told her when she held up the halter.

Oh, yeah. That was right. She'd been told that by Jarrod, the man who was supposed to mentor her through the process. He'd shown her how to halter a horse yesterday. Obviously, she hadn't been paying attention too well. She flipped the thing around.

"Not that way," Colton said with a small shake of his handsome head. She hated overly attractive men. They always made her feel so…so uncomfortable.

"The hole goes over the nose," he added. "The long strap buckles behind the horse's ears."

"Right…" she murmured.

"Here." The stall gate, which was on rollers, whooshed open like supermarket doors. "I'll do it for you."

"No, no," she said quickly, her feet bogged down in wood chips once again. He was tall. That was another thing she didn't like. Tall men intimidated the hell out of her. Jarrod, the registered hippotherapist she was working with, was short and blond. She could deal with short and blond.

She could deal with *this,* too. "I can do it."

She heard the stall door close with a bang just the same, and the sound startled Flash.

What followed was not Amber's proudest moment.

She shrieked; the horse turned away from her. The back end of the animal bashed into the wall with a boom, sending dust and debris down from the rafters. Her feet became entangled in the wood chips again. She started to fall….

He kept her from going down with a hand against her shoulder.

"Sorry about that," he told her. "I didn't think it would close so easily."

You idiot, she wanted to say. But he wasn't paying attention to her, anyway. Flash was now dancing around the stall as if Amber was a monster.

"Don't move," Colton told her. "Easy there."

Easy? There was nothing easy about this horse. The iron-shod animal had to be at least six feet tall.

"You okay?" he asked.

"I don't mean to sound panicked, but shouldn't we get out of here while the getting's good?"

He appeared to be sizing her up. "We'll be fine," he said, stepping toward the horse.

Over her shoulder, she could see that the brown beast was back to eyeing her nervously. Its swishing tail sounded like a jump rope in motion.

"No offense," she said, "but are you sure you're qualified to give direction to nonhorsey people?" After all, it was his fault the animal was acting up.

She saw Colton's eyebrows rise. They were a little too thick for her taste. "I've spent a lot of time on ranches."

"And I've spent a lot of time in a city. Doesn't mean I know how to teach people to drive."

One side of his mouth lifted in a cowboy smile— which was more of a smirk. "Point taken. I've ridden horses my entire life. I'm comfortable sharing what I know."

"In that case," she said. "I'm really glad to meet you, Colton. I'm Amber Brooks."

"Colt," he quickly corrected. "And I know. You're an intern here. You're learning to become a hippotherapist."

"I'm actually one of the camp's speech therapists, too. Hippotherapy is just something I'm hoping to study while I'm here."

He was giving her that look again. The one that made her want to wiggle like a worm on a hook. "Don't take this wrong, but you sure you want to work with horses?"

"No."

"No?"

She turned toward Flash, releasing a sigh. How to explain her life? How to explain about Dee, the nephew she loved so much? How to explain the situation with Dee's dad? That Sharron was dead, and that Dee's father was in jail…because he'd killed her sister. Not intentionally, but just about.

"It's complicated," she said.

And she shouldn't explain, anyway. The fact was Dee had been enrolled in Camp Cowboy this season, and the only one who knew that was the camp director, Gil. Amber planned to keep it that way, too.

"Try me," he said.

She shook her head. "No, seriously, it's not worth getting into. I just want to learn about horses. Hippotherapy intrigues me."

And there he went, staring at her again. It was

the oddest sort of look. As if he was trying to peel back the rind of a pomegranate, to get to the ruby-red seeds beneath. "You don't look like *any* kind of therapist," he mused.

"That's because I left my thick-framed glasses in my room."

He smirked again. "So you mind me asking why someone who doesn't know a thing about horses, and who doesn't want to become a hippotherapist, is trying to put a halter on one?"

She had to turn away.

"I'm an equine intern. That means I'll be lending a hand with the kids throughout the next few weeks. That means working with horses, obviously, so I need to get used to them. The horses, I mean."

She sneezed before she could stop herself. The horse's head popped up, and she braced herself for impact.

Nothing happened.

Flash returned to nuzzling the ground, apparently intrigued with something it found there. Ah. Food.

"Should I bother it while it's eating?"

"Nope. Horses are always looking for something to munch. If you wait for him to stop, you'll be standing there all day."

Damn, but his accent was really Southern. "If you say so." She gave Flash the same look she used when dealing with a petulant child. "Horse, prepare to be haltered."

Colt almost laughed.

Almost.

He hadn't laughed in years, or so it seemed. Not since…well, a lifetime ago.

"Easy there," said the woman he'd been told was the most dishonest piece of work this side of the Mississippi.

Standing in a beam of sunlight, she looked like an angel. One of those made-in-Taiwan Christmas tree toppers, the kind with masses and masses of fake blond ringlets. Except her hair was real. He took in the bloom of color across her cheeks. Her tipped up nose. Plump lower lip.

Gorgeous.

"Shit."

"What?" she asked, turning toward him. "Am I doing something wrong?"

"No," he said. *Get a grip, Colt. You've seen beautiful women before.* "Just walk on up to him. Trust me, he knows what you want to do."

She didn't look like a criminal.

But Logan, his best friend, swore up and down that she'd stolen his son. Hidden the boy—her nephew—away in some kind of boarding school, and she wouldn't tell Logan where he was. Didn't *have* to tell him because she had full custody of the child, thanks to Logan's brush with the law and her sister's death. From what Colt knew of her, she was a deceitful city dweller with the morals of a snake.

And so Colt had built up an idea of what Amber Brooks would look like—and this wasn't it.

She was just about to put the halter on the horse when she sneezed again. The gelding started; Amber darted away. "Okay, that does it," she said. "I'll never make it as an intern if this keeps up."

"You can't back off now," he said. "The horse will think he's won."

It might have been a few years since he'd worked his father's ranch, and he might have been young back then, but when you were dealing with animals, you wanted to be in control.

"I'm scared," she admitted. "Seriously, I think I should wait for Jarrod. He's the person I'm interning with, and when he helped me out yesterday, I wasn't half as scared."

"That's because he was standing right behind you," Colt said, moving up next to her and urging her forward with his hand. "And I can, too."

She was short, no more than five-three, with enough curves to fill a road map. But his buddy had warned him that Amber Brooks was a real piece of work. He'd known Logan since high school and was inclined to believe his friend. She might look heaven sent, but she was no angel.

"Here," he said. *Damn it.* "It goes like this." He demonstrated how to hold the halter, how to put the horse's nose in first, than how to slip the crown piece through the brass buckle. "See?"

"Oh, yeah, that's right," she said. "I remember

now. It's like the harness that people use for bondage."

Colt froze.

"Not that I'm into bondage or anything!" she quickly exclaimed, and if he read her body language right, she couldn't believe she'd said the words. "I did a paper on fetishes when I was working on my masters."

"Uh-huh."

So. She was highly educated. Probably thought she was better than everyone else.

"Thanks," she said, wry amusement on her face. "Honestly, I feel like an idiot."

"You'll do fine next time," he found himself saying. "Let's go."

"Where?" she asked.

"I was told to help you saddle up the horse. That you were wanting to learn how to ride."

"Ride?" she repeated, her blue eyes suddenly huge. "Oh, I—uh…"

He waited, wondering what the deal was with her. Why was she at this camp if she didn't know anything about horses? *She* was the reason *he'd* taken the job. It was a deal he couldn't refuse. In exchange for locating Logan's son, Colt would receive the papers on his buddy's best roping horse—an animal that'd been sitting around for a few years, sure, but a damn good horse all the same. The gelding was just the ticket Colt needed. A tie-down roper was only as good as the animal he rode, and for the past few years, Colt hadn't been that good.

"Well," he said, "the only way to learn is by working with them. Go get me a lead rope."

"Is that the long cord thingy?" she asked.

He nodded. He needed to get to know her better. To put her at ease. To become her friend.

She came back into the stall, lead rope in hand.

He snapped the rope to the horse's halter.

She was temptation wrapped in denim, and that presented a hell of a problem. He planned on betraying this pretty little package one day soon.

Chapter Two

Ride, Amber thought with a gulp.

She realized in that instant that it was one thing to decide to become a hippotherapist, quite another to actually do it…especially when horses were involved.

"Go on," Colt said, motioning her ahead of him.

He didn't look happy. She wondered if men like him found it tedious to teach newbies like her. His expression was as dour as a thundercloud.

"Where should I take her?" She glanced up at Flash.

"It's a him," the cowboy said. "There's a rack out in front of the stable. Tie him out there."

It was as if a really scary monster was following on her heels; that's what leading a horse felt like.

Get used to it, Amber. A horse might be just what Dee needs. And if that proved true, well, she'd buy him ten horses.

Colt appeared unfazed by his surroundings. How nice to have been born on a ranch. Maybe if she'd been born on one, too, she wouldn't feel so dang scared.

"How long have you been in the horse business?"

"Long time," he said.

They stepped out of the shelter of the barn, and after being inside for so long, Amber had to blink in the glaring sunlight. It was bright outside, but so beautiful. Tall trees framed a parklike setting. She was pretty sure the trees were redwoods, they were so huge. In the distance she could see the empty army barracks. It seemed sad that up until last year the place had been abandoned. Well, now the Golden State Therapeutic Center, aka Camp Cowboy, made good use of it.

"No," Colt said. "Not like that."

Amber glanced down at the cord she'd wrapped around a pole.

She'd been so deep in thought she hadn't given a second thought to how she tied it. "Not like what?"

"You need to use a quick-release knot."

"Uh…how do I do that?" Jarrod hadn't taught her that yesterday. The good-looking blond staffer had simply taken the lead from her and done it himself.

"Like this." Colt stepped toward her. Surely some football team in the South was lamenting the loss of such an athletic looking guy. "See?"

No, Amber hadn't seen. They stood in front of a hitching post that looked a lot like the ones in Western movies. Apparently, there hadn't been a lot of technological advances in horse hitching recently.

But what he did with that rope might as well have been cat's cradle. "Can you do that again?"

"Wrap it around once," he said. "Then cross over, then make a loop, then pull the end through the loop. See?"

"I think I do," she said. But it quickly became apparent that she didn't see at all.

"Here," he said, taking her hands in his. He had a really huge one. Ginormous. She felt like Fay Wray in King Kong's palm.

"Wrap it around once, cross the two strands, slip the loop through the V here." He demonstrated, then slid the loose end through the resulting loop.

"Oh!" At last she got it. Though why they needed a special way to tie horses was anybody's guess.

"It's so you can release the rope quickly if he pulls back."

Had she really been that easy to read?

"Got it," she said. "Although I'm not sure I want to know what 'pulling back' means in horseydom."

"I don't expect that to happen with any of the animals here. As I understand it, they've all been therapy horses for at least a year."

"That's a relief. I was thinking I might need to update my life insurance policy."

There he went, staring at her again. "You'll be fine," he stated simply.

"Good to know," she murmured. "Now what?"

"Well, I assume there are some grooming brushes around here?"

what the National Finals Rodeo was. She did because Logan had almost made it one year. In hindsight things had started to fall apart when he'd failed to make the mark.

"Not yet," Colt said. "Next year."

Jarrod huffed, conveying all too clearly, *Yeah, that's what they all say.*

"Well, I better head up to Gil's office," Amber said.

"I'll walk with you," Jarrod announced.

"You coming back?" Colt asked before she could turn away.

"Depends on what Gil wants."

Colt's eyes narrowed. Amber knew exactly what he was thinking.

Chicken.

"YOU NEEDED TO SEE ME?" Amber said, entering Gil's office tentatively. The way he was bent over his massive oak desk, she could see the horseshoe of hair around his shiny pate.

"Amber," he said, pushing his wire-rimmed glasses back up his nose. "Come on in."

They were in a centuries-old lodge, one that had been erected to house cavalry offices well over a hundred years ago. Frankly, it amazed Amber that the place was still standing, but it had been crafted in an era when things were made to last. Vaulted ceilings. Crown molding. Wood-paneled walls. The four-story building had been meticulously maintained by the County of San Francisco, and that was a good thing. It would have been a shame to let such a treasure go to waste. That had been Camp Cowboy's selling point to the county when they'd wanted to lease the building. Apparently. As a newbie, she was still piecing together this business and how it could exist on the Presidio grounds.

"What's up?" she asked.

"Have a seat," he said.

Gil's office was on the bottom floor, to the left of the entrance, in a room Amber suspected had been occupied by the base commander years and years ago—or whatever the cavalry equivalent of that was. Wood-framed windows offered a stunning view of the park outside. Off in the distance was a grove of trees, and just above that, barely noticeably unless you knew what you were looking for, the tall spires of the Golden Gate Bridge.

"I received a call today," Gil said, leaning back and making a steeple out of his fingers.

There was a chair in front of his desk. Amber sank into it. "Oh, yeah?" But she knew.

"It was from Pelican Bay."

Her shoulders slumped. "He *phoned* here?"

"Care to tell me what's going on?"

She hadn't told Gil about Dee's father. Hadn't wanted to tell him. It was her own personal skeleton. All the camp director knew was that she had sole custody of her nephew. That Dee's father was out of the picture.

"Who is *he?*" Gil asked.

"My nephew's father," Amber admitted.

The edges of Gil's eyes crinkled as he gave that some thought. "So this is what you meant by out of the picture?"

She nodded. "He was incarcerated for involuntary manslaughter."

Of her sister. Sharron.

And it made her physically ill to think about it. To be pulled back to that night. The call from the police. The drive to the hospital. The doctor gently breaking the news.

Frankly, jail had been too kind a punishment for her ex-brother-in-law.

"When will he get out?" Gil asked.

"He was given a five year sentence. He has two years left to serve." But he had a parole hearing in another month. They might actually let the bastard out. And then he would fight her for custody of Dee. He'd already told her that. But she would never let that happen. She would not allow the man who killed her sister to kill her sister's child, too.

"Okay," Gil said. "So I should expect calls from him?"

"I told him not to phone me," she said. "But he's been demanding to know where Dee is."

"You mean he doesn't know?"

She shook her head. "Early on, he would call Dee. When Dee wouldn't talk to him, he would get belligerent, start yelling." And her poor nephew didn't do well with that. Not at all. "It would upset Dee," she explained. "I told the facility not to take his calls anymore, but when Dee's father started making threats against the workers there…" Gosh, she hated airing her dirty laundry. "It was just easier to move Dee to a new home, especially once we figured out he was nonverbal. He's been at Little Voices ever since, and he's doing well. His father doesn't need to know anything more than that."

But one day he would be out of jail.

She closed her eyes, refusing to think of that.

"This is hard on you, isn't it?" Gil asked.

She shrugged, trying to make light of the situation, but it was a sham. "It kills me some days," she admitted. "But I have to have Dee's best interest at heart."

Gil seemed satisfied with the answer. "Well, I'll tell the switchboard to put all calls through to you."

"Thank you," she said. "And if you could please make sure nobody knows Dee is my nephew…"

"Confidentiality is the policy of this facility," Gil said sternly.

"Yes, of course." She was counting on that.

"But I do wonder if telling his father that Dee is here with you might be a good thing. Surely he would settle down if you told him the lengths you've gone though to help his son."

"No," she said. "I tried that route before. Dee's father doesn't trust me. He thinks I hate him."

And she did…didn't she?

No. She didn't hate anybody. She just didn't trust him. He might make claims that he'd changed, but she knew that wasn't true. A leopard didn't change its spots.

"Well then," Gil said, "I'll respect your need for privacy."

"Thank you."

"But if this doesn't work out, if your nephew doesn't respond to therapy like you hope, what will you do then?"

She'd thought about that at least a half dozen times since taking a leave of absence from work to train at Camp Cowboy. What if this was a mistake? What if Dee didn't respond to horse therapy as she hoped?

"Either way, learning a little about hippotherapy is a good thing," she said. "Who knows where it might take me?" She glanced down at her lap for a moment. "And I'll do whatever it takes to help my nephew. If this doesn't work out…" she shrugged again. "Well, I'll just try something else."

Gil nodded, smiling. "Good. I'm glad you're not looking at this like it might be an answer to your prayers. One never knows how an autistic child will respond."

"I know."

"Then I wish you luck," he said, standing.

Luck. Yeah, she *would* need that.

Chapter Three

She was in a meeting, Colt thought, heart pounding, as he put Flash away. He would never have a better opportunity to search through her belongings than right now.

But the idea filled him with a sense of anxiety and dread.

His fingers shook as he unclipped Flash's halter. The camp wasn't fully staffed yet. He'd been told most of the live-ins would arrive tomorrow. That meant fewer people around today.

He had to investigate now.

His stomach roiled as he left the stables. "The lodge," as staffers called it, looked like it belonged on a dollar bill: Georgian-style roof, sash windows, wide steps leading up to the entrance. It had been built on a slight incline, with a pebbled road leading up to it. Those employees who would be driving in Monday would park around back, but for now, the place looked deserted.

Colt took the steps two at a time, feeling sick with trepidation. The lodge had double doors at the entrance, but only the right side worked. Colt saw movement on the other side of the frosted glass. He knew Gil's office was to the left, and when he stepped inside, that door was closed.

Good. Amber was still in her meeting.

"That was fast."

Colt jerked his gaze to the right, to find Jim or Jerry or whatever his name was sitting there. In the cafeteria, actually, although the spacious room with the hardwood floors looked more like a ballroom, except for the tables and chairs.

"No reason to stick around at the stables if there's nothing to do." The horse therapist Amber had introduced him to earlier looked skeptical.

"Don't you have to feed stock or something?"

The guy—Jarrod, he suddenly remembered—was obnoxious. Colt had no idea what he'd done to garner such animosity, but it was obvious they hadn't hit it off. "Not for another hour," he said, moving past the cafeteria without another word. There was an elevator in the left-hand corner of the foyer—a recent addition by the looks of it. He ignored it and took the steps directly ahead. The staff would all be living coed style, which, for all he knew, meant Amber could be bunking right next to him.

She wasn't.

He checked the room chart hanging at the end of the hall. Room seven. He was in room three, which meant he had to walk by his own room, which meant—

Woof!

"Mac," Colt warned. "Quiet."

But his dog had caught his scent. White-and-black paws scratched at the door. Colt could just make them out through the crack. Terrific. He'd insisted the animal wouldn't be a problem, but Gil had warned that if Mac disturbed any of the residents, Colt would have to board him at a kennel—an option he couldn't afford.

"Quiet!" He glanced left and right as he walked on. A few of the doors were open, but he didn't see anyone. The place reminded him of a hospital ward. *Utilitarian* was the word. No frills here.

Her door was closed.

He peeked over his shoulder, grateful that nobody was around, but when it came time to actually grasp the doorknob, he hesitated.

Woof.

"Mac," he called out. He opened the door and stepped inside before he could change his mind. If someone heard his dog and came to investigate, they'd see him standing there. Not good. But once inside her room, he froze.

He hated this.

Just do it.

Forcing himself to relax, he scanned her room. Bed to his left. Table and chairs to his right. There was a purse sitting on the brown seat, clearly open.

Go.

But he couldn't. He wasn't cut out for this, he realized. The idea of rummaging through her things…

He just couldn't do it. He swung around, and came face-to-face with Amber.

"What the heck are you doing in here?" she said, her blue eyes wide with surprise.

"I…uh…" Damn it. He couldn't think. "I wanted to apologize."

"Apologize? For what?"

"Earlier," he improvised. And he hated it. Lying wasn't in his nature. "For forcing you to get on Flash."

"You didn't force me," she said, crossing her arms. "I didn't ride at all." With the window behind him and the sunlight pouring over her, her eyes seemed to glow. As did her hair. He found himself forgetting for a moment what he'd come here to do.

"You would have if we hadn't been interrupted. And I was pushy about the whole thing."

"I didn't notice," she said, but he knew she lied.

Colt shook his head, hoping she didn't see guilt on his face. "I, uh, I spend a lot of time working out of doors. With men. On ranches. I guess I just forgot you weren't one of my crew." That, at least, was true. So far he hadn't lied to her. Not really. And he hadn't rummaged through her belongings.

"You don't have a girlfriend?"

"No," he said quickly.

Her lips twitched, as if she was about to ask him a question, but she must have changed her mind.

"Do you have a boyfriend?" he asked, to fill the quiet.

Now why'd you go and say that?

"Boyfriend?" She laughed. "Hah. Who has time for that? Between my job and my…"

He waited for her to say the word *nephew*.

"…crazy life," she said instead, "I don't have time for sleep, much less a boyfriend."

"Your life's crazy?"

But she wasn't budging. He could see that. "It is," she said, swinging open the door pointedly. "Anyway, apology accepted."

"Can we try again tomorrow?"

She raised her eyebrows. "You mean ride?"

He nodded.

She licked her lips. And suddenly he found himself thinking less about subterfuge and more about the shape of those lips.

"Let me think about it," she said.

He didn't move, even though it was obvious she wanted him to leave. But he couldn't do that. If he couldn't bring himself to rummage through her belongings, he needed to come up with some other way to get the information out of her.

"Don't chew it over too long," he said, forcing himself to smile. "Tomorrow's Sunday. From what I hear, things are going to get crazy on Monday." He walked to the door, but didn't leave. He turned to face her, effectively imprisoning her between his body and the wall.

"I want to help you," he said.

"You do?"

Man, she was a pretty little thing. He couldn't keep from staring at her mouth. "Let me coach you some more."

She chewed the inside of her lip. She looked adorable when she did that. Like a kid trying to determine if she wanted vanilla ice cream or chocolate.

"What time were you thinking?" she asked.

"Maybe around ten or so?" he said, cursing inwardly. She was not to be trusted. "I'm supposed to do some things around the barn tomorrow. So after that?"

She seemed to think about it for a moment. "All right. Tomorrow."

"See you then," he said, because he knew if he didn't leave right then, he might do something he would regret. And that wouldn't be good. Logan had told him exactly how horrible this woman really was.

SEE YOU THEN.

Lord, her sister would be laughing her head off if she knew the direction of Amber's thoughts.

A cowboy.

"Brother," she murmured, dropping onto the bed.

But she didn't get much sleep that night. She told herself she could bug out on Colt, maybe go down and try to halter and work with Flash on her own. But that would be silly. She didn't want to get hurt. She wanted to learn.

The other option was asking Jarrod, but something about the guy's attitude really rubbed her the wrong way. At least Colt seemed genuine.

So she showed up in her jeans and a sweatshirt. While the day had dawned overcast and cold—typical January weather—the fog had burned off, leaving bright blue skies behind, although it was still a bit chilly. When she arrived at the stables, she was startled to see Flash already tied out front, and that Colt wasn't alone.

"Mac," he called to the dog, which stood up when he saw her.

"You have a *dog?*" she asked in shock.

"I do."

"Hey, there," she said, squatting.

"Mac!"

But the dog didn't listen. As if he'd been waiting for just such an invitation, he charged.

"Damn it, Mac!"

But Amber didn't mind. She held out her arms, thoroughly enchanted with the gray-black-and-brown animal. He had no tail. It'd been cropped at some point, but that didn't stop his rear end from swinging back and forth.

"What kind of dog is he?"

"Australian shepherd," Colt said. "And I'm about to deport him back to his homeland." He stomped forward.

"No, it's okay," she said, staving him off with a hand. "I love dogs."

"You do?"

"I do," she exclaimed, plunging her hands into the shepherd's thick fur and giving him a good scratch. Mac fairly moaned. "Such pretty eyes," she cooed. They were blue. Blue like the water in Crater Lake. "But where have you been keeping him?"

"In my room," he said. "Gil told me that was okay as long as he didn't cause trouble."

"What?" she said in mock surprise. "Mac, cause trouble? Nah." She smiled at the animal.

When she stood up, she found Colt staring at her, and she felt self-conscious all of a sudden. "I see you got Flash ready."

"Uh, yeah. Hope you don't mind. I didn't see any good reason to torture you by making you halter the animal. I want you to enjoy yourself today."

"Thanks," she said, her relief so great she almost hugged him.

"Come on, Mac."

"Where are you putting him?"

"In one of the empty stalls. I don't want him getting under your feet. Go on in and get some brushes," Colt added. "I'll be right back."

She did so, thinking *In for a penny, in for a pound.*

"Don't those hard bristles hurt?" she asked when he came back out.

"No, not like that." Colt took the brush from her hand. She felt the jolt of their fingers meeting like a static charge.

"And horses actually like it," he said.

As he moved closer, Amber found herself wanting to edge away.

"Use long strokes," Colt instructed, his gaze hooking her own. "Start at his neck and work your way back. Sometimes it's easier to use a currycomb first. That'll knock the hair loose."

"And a currycomb looks like…what, exactly?"

Colt bent and pulled something out of the bucket that caused her to say, "Ouch. Now *that* can't feel good." It looked like a lollipop, only the "pop" part was made of metal. And it had teeth. Sharp, pointed teeth.

"You'd be surprised what feels good to a horse."

She eyed the animal. "Actually, given that I know absolutely nothing about them, I don't think anything would surprise me. How do I use the currycomb?"

"Move it in circular patterns."

She nodded. "Wax on. Wax off."

"Excuse me?"

"*Karate Kid.* Haven't you ever seen that movie?"

Colt stared down at her as if he'd never heard of anything remotely related to karate—movies or otherwise—in his life, but that didn't dissuade her.

"Sensei tell you to wax on, wax off," she said.

But all Colt did was stare. The man was about as warm and as friendly as Mount Everest.

"Once you're done," he said, "follow up with the brush. I'm going to go get the tack."

She gave the brush a hard flick, and was immediately rewarded by a cloud of dust and dander. She coughed, waving a hand in front of her face, although the smell of horse wasn't all that unpleasant. And the animal seemed to have calmed down. His head hung low, his brown eyes half-closed, as if he was falling asleep at the hitching post. Hmm. Maybe this wouldn't be as scary as she thought.

"You done?"

"No," Amber said in exasperation. "And please don't sneak up on me like that."

Colt dropped the saddle and hung the bridle on the end of the post Flash was tied to. "Here," he said, "I'll do the other side."

And that was how Amber found herself quietly grooming a horse—because Mr. Colt Sheridan appeared to be the tall, dark and *silent* type. But that was okay. It gave her time to think.

Dee would be arriving soon, although no one could make the connection. Her nephew's birth certificate said Rudolph, a result of Sharron's twisted sense of humor, when he'd been born on Christmas Day. But everybody, including his father, called him Rudy, and that suited Amber just fine. Logan had been begging to see him again, and Amber just couldn't do that to her nephew. The last time they'd been to visit it had been so horrible. Dee had gone into meltdown. Logan had grown irate. The supervising officer had had to intervene.... Horrible. All the proof she needed that her brother-in-law hadn't changed, not one whit.

"So what made you want to work with special needs children?"

She again waved a hand in front of her face as dust tickled her nose. "It's a long story."

Colt continued grooming Flash, although she could swear he was trying to denude the beast. Dander and hair were flying. Thank goodness she wasn't allergic to horses.

"I've got all the time in the world," he said, his eyes meeting hers for a moment.

"No, really," she said.

"You like kids, don't you?"

"Of course I do," she answered quickly.

"Do you want any of your own?"

He hadn't stopped brushing, but she could feel him glancing at her. Every time he did, it was like warm flashes of sunlight touched her—which, honestly, was a strange thing to think.

"Someday," she said. "How about you? What made you want to work for Camp Cowboy?"

"I didn't."

That made her stop brushing for a second. "Excuse me?"

"I heard about this place from a friend. He told me I should apply. So I did."

She didn't know why that stunned her, but it did. She'd just assumed everyone who worked at Camp Cowboy had done so out of a need to serve. To make the world a better place. To reach out and maybe help a child.

Her life's mission, thanks to Dee.

"So if your friend hadn't suggested you apply, you'd have...what?"

He shrugged. "I don't know what I would have done for cash. Found something else."

"But you wanted to work with special needs kids, didn't you?"

She could tell he didn't want to answer her question because his eyes flicked over Flash as he groomed, then to her, then back again. "My first love is rodeo," he admitted.

Of course. She should have known.

Just like her sister's husband.

Amber was certain the rodeo lifestyle had corrupted Logan to the point of no return. Cowboys boozed it up and chased women. That's what her sister said, and Amber believed it. "I know someone who used to do that."

"Yeah?" Colt asked.

But she wasn't ready to answer questions about Dee's father, even though she was curious if the two knew each other. The man was better off gone from their lives, something that was hard to explain to strangers.

"Please tell me you at least *like* kids?" she replied, trying to change the subject.

He paused. "Kids and I don't get along."

Her body turned into a pillar of salt—or so it felt. "What the heck are you doing here then?"

He looked her right in the eye. She watched as he tried to find the words. In the end he simply shrugged and said, "Searching for something."

Chapter Four

Now why the heck had he gone and said that? he wondered, flicking the brush over Flash's back harder than necessary. Flash pinned his ears, and Cold patted his rump in apology.

"Searching for what?" she asked, clearly curious.

"I don't know," he hedged, then shrugged. "But the rodeo life, it's getting hard."

That's why he *had* to do this. Time was running out—and she was his ticket to the big leagues.

"So quit," she suggested.

"No," he said. "Not yet."

Because he could still do this thing. He just needed to figure out a way to discover where Rudy was without feeling like a complete jerk in the process.

You are *a jerk.*

Amber was shaking her head, and he could tell she didn't like his answer. Not only that, but she almost appeared disappointed.

"Okay," she said brightly—too brightly. "What's next?"

He wondered if he should push the issue. Ask her about the guy she knew on the rodeo circuit. Logan. It had to be Logan. It was the perfect way to get her to talk. That's what he *should* do. Instead, he found himself gesturing with his chin. "Saddle first, then bridle."

"And how do you do that?"

"Here." He scooped up the saddle blanket. "This goes on first." He made sure it was placed squarely. "Then the saddle," he said, swinging it onto the horse's back.

"How come I have this feeling it's a lot harder than it looks?"

He pulled the saddle off and demonstrated again. But the whole time he worked with her, he found himself wondering if Logan might be wrong about her. Was that possible? Was there more to the story than met the eye? And why the hell did Colt keep thinking about his ranch all of a sudden? He hadn't been back to Texas in years, not since he was seventeen....

Don't go down that road again, buddy.

"Is that thing going in there?" she asked.

They'd reached the part where it was time to bridle the horse. Colt realized it was the bit she was staring at.

"It is," he said, telling himself to smile. Except he couldn't bring himself to do much more than say, "Don't worry. Doesn't hurt. He knows the deal.

Watch." He showed her how Flash had been taught to take the bit.

Could Logan be wrong? Or worse, lying?

Damn it. Colt wished he could just ask.

"Doesn't that hurt?" she asked when the metal clunked against the gelding's teeth.

"Only if you don't know what you're doing," he said. *Just focus on what you're here to do.* "But you will," he quickly reassured her. "Here. I'll show you." Because that's what he'd been hired to do—help out with the horses.

"Can I try?" she asked.

"Sure." He slipped the bridle off again and handed it to her.

Just tough it out.

When the camp closed in eight weeks, it was back to rodeo—with his pockets full and a new horse to ride.

"Hold it from the top," he instructed when she looked at the bridle, baffled. She moved the bit close to Flash's mouth, but when the gelding jerked his head back, she jumped as if he'd tried to bite her.

"You know, I'm starting to think you don't like horses," Colt said.

"I don't."

He thought he misheard her. "Excuse me?"

"They intimidate the hell out of me."

"Then what the heck are *you* doing here?" he found himself asking.

She looked at the animal, then at the stable where

he'd come from. "This is the wave of the future," she said. "Or at least that's what research shows. There have been studies recently, really amazing studies, that prove an animal can connect with special needs children in a way that defies explanation. I *have* to do this."

"Why?"

She flicked her chin up. "Because."

Was it because of her nephew? Logan had admitted his son wasn't quite "normal," but said he just had a learning disability. Was that what drove Amber's passion?

"If you don't want to be afraid of horses, you need to realize something."

"What's that?" she asked, the bridle in her hand forgotten.

"They're like dogs."

"Excuse me?"

"Like a gigantic Mac," Colt amended. "Really. Most horses are just as smart as Mac in there— sometimes smarter."

As if his dog had been listening, Amber heard him yelp.

"Is he okay?"

"He's fine. He just wants to be out with us."

"That'd be okay with me."

"No," Colt said. "You need to focus on what I'm saying."

"I am paying attention," she said, eyeing the horse. "What you just told me was not to worry. That if a horse wants to kill me, it's smart enough to know the best way to accomplish that goal."

Against his better judgment, he smiled, but only for a moment. "Horses don't want to kill humans. I've seen half a dozen jump over a rider unfortunate enough to land in front of them."

She tipped her head sideways, her ringlets hanging over her shoulder like a bunch of grapes. "Yes, but how did that rider get in front of those horses in the first place?"

"At rodeos cowboys fall off all the time. As a matter of fact, it's what I do for a living—jump off horses."

"What do you mean?"

"I'm a tie-down roper."

"What's that?"

"Someone who jumps off a running horse and wrestles steers to the ground."

"And you do that why?"

It's a living.

They were the first words to come to mind, even though he knew well and good there were easier ways to do that. Hell, he worked ranches during the off season. He *owned* a ranch. But full-time ranching? Nah. That'd been his dad's deal. And his mom's. And his baby sister's—

Colt snatched the bridle from Amber. "Sorry," he said when she looked up at him in surprise. "Let's just get you mounted. That way you can see for yourself there's nothing to fear."

And he could get out of here.

"Find yourself a helmet," he snapped.

"Helmet? You think I might fall off?"

"No," he said. "It's a safety precaution. I was told everyone here rides with a helmet."

He wasn't cut out for this, he decided. Dealing with her while trying to keep quiet about why he was actually at Camp Cowboy. And then there was this…this whatever it was that reminded him of his family and the life he used to live.

"Do you know where the helmets are?" she asked.

"Never mind," he said. "I'll go get one."

He thrust the reins at her. But as he walked into the barn, blinking in the sudden dimness, he wondered if maybe it wouldn't have to be so difficult. And maybe he wouldn't have to lie to her. Maybe he could discover some other way to unearth her nephew's location.

Because even though he wanted to help his buddy, he wasn't at all convinced he had what it took to do. *She* might be a deceitful you-know-what, but *he* wasn't. And that might present a problem.

HE'D GONE ALL QUIET on her. Since they'd walked to the arena together, helmet in hand, he'd said hardly two words to her.

"Climb on board," he said.

Okay, make that four. "Sure," she said. "If you tell me how."

He looked at her as if butterflies were spitting

out of her mouth. "Haven't you ever seen someone getting on a horse before?"

He seemed angry. Or frustrated. Or…something. "Haven't you ever worked with beginners before?" she retorted.

He didn't answer her.

"Haven't you?" she pressed.

"No," he finally admitted.

That got her attention. "Then how the heck did you get this job?"

"Frankly, I don't know. Luck, I guess."

"No way," she said.

"I faxed in a résumé last Monday, had a phone interview on Tuesday. They did a background check and verified my references by Thursday and here I am today."

Today being Sunday. But she'd known Gil and Buck had been desperate to find someone to help out. Scuttlebutt was that finding qualified horse personnel in the middle of San Francisco had been a challenge, especially someone willing to work with special needs children.

"So this is your first time teaching people to ride?"

He nodded. "And so I guess we *all* have something to learn."

She squared off with Flash. "Well, all right then. Tell me what to do, cowboy."

He crossed his arms, the motion highlighting the

muscular bulge of his biceps. She liked the way his shirt hugged him, emphasizing how fit he was.

"Okay," he said after a moment's pause, as if he'd been mentally gearing himself up for the task, too. "Put your left foot in the stirrup."

"And my right foot out?"

She could have sworn he fought back a smile.

"So after the left foot, then what?"

"Grab the saddle horn and pull yourself up."

He made it sound sooo easy.

It was not.

She felt as if she was playing a game of Twister. Once she managed to get her foot into the stirrup, it slipped out the minute she went to grab the saddle horn. Forget about pulling herself up.

"This is impossible," she said. "You'd have to be double-jointed to get close enough to drag yourself onto a horse's back."

"Try facing the front of the animal," he said.

Amazingly, that seemed to do the trick. But even after getting her foot into the stirrup and taking a firm hold of the saddle, she couldn't pull herself up.

"I'm too fat," she muttered.

"You are *not* fat," she heard him pronounce.

"Easy for you to say. You're not the one trying to pull it all up."

"You are not fat," he said again.

She turned to look at him, drawing back instantly. He was right behind her. "You're the perfect weight," he stated.

Amber wondered if he was attracted to her, too. "Thanks."

"I'll help lift you up," he said.

"If that involves putting your hands on my rump, forget it."

He had an amazing smile when he chose to use it. "Just try and swing yourself up. I'll do the rest."

She thrust her foot in the stirrup, grabbed the saddle...

He did the rest.

He clasped his hands around her waist as if she were a figure skater and he was her partner. She didn't need to use the stirrup so much as clutch at the saddle. The end result was less than graceful, but before she knew it she found herself sitting on the worn leather.

Amber sighed loudly, out of breath. She could still feel where his hands had been. "And they make it look so easy on TV."

"It'll get easier," he said.

She kept clutching the saddle horn, even though she knew she should be looking around for the leather strap thingy. What did they call them? The reins. She should be holding on to the reins in case the animal beneath her—a very *big* animal—decided to bolt, or to charge, or to buck and twist to throw her off.

"Maybe it's nothing to you," she said. "But it's a big deal to me. I feel like I've conquered the world." She smiled.

"You're right. No big deal." He turned on his booted heel and began to leave.

"Hey!" she cried.

But he didn't turn back.

"Hey!" she called again, louder.

He walked away.

Chapter Five

It had happened again, Colt thought, practically running ahead of Amber.

Something about her reminded him of his mom. Or maybe his sister. One of them. So? That didn't mean anything.

"Hey," Colt heard her call again.

He told himself to walk straight past the arena gate. Hell, he should head to the parking area and get in his truck. Amber Brooks was the worst sort of woman to be attracted to. The only reason he'd met her was because he'd been sent to find out where her nephew was. She'd stolen a man's son away. Okay, so maybe not stolen. She had legal custody of the child, but the fact remained that she refused to bring Rudy by to visit his father. Refused to let Logan see his son. Refused to let Logan even talk to him on the phone.

"Okay, fine," she said. "Leave me here. But I want you to know that you're the worst damn riding instructor I've ever met."

And he was angry, he admitted. That's why he wanted to walk out.

"And that's saying a lot, since you're the only riding instructor I know."

"Crap," he muttered under his breath.

He couldn't leave her there.

He slowly swung around to face her. She had the same joy of spirit that his sister had. That's why she reminded him of Maggie.

Crap.

"Follow me," he said.

She sat on the horse like an abandoned child. "I would love to 'follow you,'" she said, "if you would only tell me how, exactly, to do that."

Get it together, Colt.

"Okay." He took a deep breath. He could quit at any moment.

And go back to day-leasing pathetic horses next year.

"First thing you need to do is pick up the reins."

She glanced down. "Reins," she said, scooping them up as if she was scooping out ice cream. "Check."

Damn it. He would have to touch her again. "Not like that," he said. "Both of them in one hand."

She looked at them, clearly confused, then switched the reins to one hand, but they were all wadded up wrong.

"No," he said. "Leave the ends hanging out."

Against his better judgment, he went over to her. "Like this."

She had petite hands. And nice nails. They weren't painted, but were well-shaped. He couldn't stand bright colors on a woman's nails. Made them look cheap.

He almost forgot to let go of her hand holding the reins until she said, "Oh, I see."

Colt stepped back, grateful for a little distance. He forced himself to remember she wasn't as sweet as she looked. Even panthers were beautiful.

"Now what?" she asked.

Mean. Arrogant. Self-righteous. Those were the words Logan had used to describe her.

"Go ahead and squeeze Flash's sides with your legs," he said.

But she didn't seem evil.

"Like this?" she asked.

Not at all.

"Harder," he said.

Her face was turning red. Colt realized she was squeezing the horse as if trying to make juice out of him.

"It's not working," she huffed.

"Try a kick."

She tapped her heels.

"Harder."

That seemed to do the trick. Flash took a step. Colt almost laughed when he caught the look on Amber's face. She couldn't have appeared more stunned, if she'd been shot off in a rocket.

"That's working better," she said, kicking harder.

The gelding flung his head up in response. "Not too hard," Colt said. "We don't want to get him upset, especially when he's moving along just fine now."

She looked pleased. And excited. And…happy.

"Lay your reins on his neck to guide him to the arena."

"What are you going to do?"

"I'll be right next to you in case you need me, but you won't."

"How do you know that?"

"That's a good horse you've got there," Colt said. He'd met Buck only once, but had been impressed with the old cowboy's horse sense.

"How do I apply the brakes?"

"Pull and lean back at the same time."

She started to do as instructed. "Not now," Colt said quickly. "Wait until you get into the arena before learning to use the control stick."

"Leave it to a man to call the reins a control stick," he heard her mutter.

Eucalyptus trees towered overhead, their shade and pungent smell pleasant. He kicked at the fallen leaves. Beyond them lay the arena, and beyond that, an open field that seemed out of place given all the trees around them. Then he remembered what it was. He'd read about it online. That was the cavalry field, where officers had practiced maneuvers on horseback. The arena had been added later, and the wood fence that surrounded the perimeter painted a brilliant white.

"Here." He moved ahead of her to open the gate. "Pull him to a stop when I get inside."

"Okeydokey."

It was a nice arena, Colt thought. Someone had spent major bucks on the place. He would give his right eye for an arena like this to use for practice. As things stood, he was forced to mooch off his friends. Drove him nuts. But the only way he could afford something like this was if he got his hands on Logan's horse, which meant getting his head out of his ass.

Colt took a deep breath.

"You have any family?" he asked, coming to a stop next to her.

If she was startled by his question, she didn't show it. "Some."

"Were you ever married?" he asked, even though he knew she wasn't. But he was trying to draw her out, get her to talk.

"No."

Too late he realized his question might be misinterpreted as interest on his part. He scanned her face, searching for evidence that she might have taken it the wrong way. She wouldn't look him in the eye.

"Any brothers or sisters?"

He'd have to have been blind not to notice the way she winced. Her sister had died in a car crash, he knew. That was how Amber had gotten custody of her nephew…when Logan had gone to jail.

"No," she said again. "Nobody."

He couldn't very well call her a liar. Although, technically, she wasn't really lying.

Kinda like you.

One step at a time. He moved back and crossed his arms. "Try a circle."

"And how does one turn?" she asked pointedly.

"Move your arm in the direction you want to go."

And that was that. Flash must have been very well trained because he listened to the halfhearted directions she gave him.

"Can I go faster?" she asked.

"Wow! First day on a horse and already she wants to go faster."

They both turned to see Gil approaching with a young couple and a child. The balding camp director looked especially out of place in such a countrylike setting, in his polyester black pants and a button-down white shirt, Colt decided. The woman with him held the hand of a little boy, who looked to be six or seven years old.

"Good to see you're having so much fun," Gil said.

"Fun?" Amber smiled widely. "This isn't fun, this is *work*. My arms are sore from brushing and my legs are weak from squeezing."

Gil smiled back at her. "Hear that, Eric? This isn't going to be all fun and games."

But the little boy didn't move. He didn't do much of anything besides look at the ground. Colt noticed that he had a prosthetic leg, and his arm was curled up against his belly.

Colt felt as if he'd been punched.

Car crash. What else would have caused these kinds of injuries?

"Amber and Colt, this is Mr. and Mrs. Peery. Despite your experience, Amber, the Peerys are hoping their son, Eric, might have fun learning to ride."

Colt turned just in time to catch Amber jumping down from her horse like a member of the Pony Express. He marveled for a moment, wondering where she'd learned that move. Her curls tumbled around her shoulders, as bright as her smile. He couldn't take his eyes off of her as she dashed forward, only to draw up abruptly when Flash didn't immediately follow.

"Come on," she told the gelding.

But the big bay was moving at his own pace. Colt interceded. "Here, I'll lead him forward."

His gaze slid to the parents. Both of them had their eyes on their child, and if Colt wasn't mistaken, the mother looked disappointed by her son's lack of interest. He watched as she lifted her free hand to touch her blond hair, then dropped it again. Her husband seemed just as on edge.

"Hi, Eric," Amber said as they drew close to Camp Cowboy's newest student. She squatted low. "My name is Amber."

He wouldn't look at her, but that didn't faze her. "Would you like to meet Flash?" she asked.

Eric edged nearer to his mom, his expression pained.

"Don't worry, he's not going to hurt you," his mother said softly. Then she glanced at Colt, telling him without words he could bring the horse closer.

"It's okay to be afraid," Amber said. "I was scared of horses at first, too. But I've learned they're really nice."

Colt led the gelding as far as he could without actually bumping into the child. Flash seemed curious, pricking his ears up and dropping his head. Colt watched as the gelding's nostrils flared, a sure sign he was trying to catch Eric's scent.

"See?" Amber said gently, reaching up to pat Flash's neck.

"Go ahead, son," the father said. "You can pet him, too."

Tentatively, the kid reached out with his good arm. Colt saw the scars there—multiple angry red lines that could only result from deep gashes.

He had to force himself not to turn away.

"Hey, horsey." Eric glanced up at his parents, wonder in his face.

"Would you like to ride him?" Amber asked.

Eric looked from his dad to his mom.

"I don't have a problem with that," Mrs. Peery said. "If you think it's safe."

"It's an excellent idea," Gil said. "Colt here can help him up."

"I'll get him a child-size helmet," Amber said, dashing off eagerly.

Colt stared at those scars.

"Drunk driver," Eric's mom said in a low voice, next to him. Her son was busy stroking the horse, her husband squatting down behind him. "We were on our way to a baseball game."

She shook her head, her eyes red.

"Three in the afternoon and the man's triple the legal limit."

"I'm sorry," Colt said, but he was frozen inside. He wanted to leave.

"Here we go," Amber said breathlessly, handing over the helmet.

Mr. Peery took it from her and helped his son put it on.

"You ready?" Amber asked in a bright voice.

Eric nodded.

"Okay, here we go." She took the reins from Colt, who guided the child to the horse's side. He weighed next to nothing when Colt swung him into the saddle.

Drunk driver.

Had the driver lived? If so, did he suffer from the crushing burden of his guilt?

"You okay up there?" the little boy's mother asked him.

The child wore a grin on his face that stretched across his entire face.

Colt busied himself adjusting the stirrups.

"Mom, Dad," Amber said, "can you take up a position on either side?"

Then Colt stepped away, and Amber began to lead the horse forward. Eric's grin went supernova. He clutched the saddle horn with his good hand, his giggle causing everyone around him to smile.

Except Colt.

"You okay?" Gil asked.

Colt hadn't realized he'd stopped moving and that the director had come up next to him. "I'm fine," he forced himself to say. "Just watching."

But he was far from fine.

Chapter Six

Something was wrong with Colt, Amber thought as she led Flash around.

It took every ounce of her resolve not to turn and ask him what was up, but her focus had to be on Eric and helping him to stay on the horse. And it was funny, too, because she didn't feel half as uncomfortable around Flash today as she had yesterday.

"You're doing great, Eric," his father said.

"I can't believe it," Mrs. Peery added. "You're riding. I didn't think you'd do that for at least a week."

"Normally he wouldn't," Amber said, glancing at Colt again. "Usually, we spend a week or more just getting kids used to being around horses, but I've never heard of a pony ride hurting someone. Not," she added quickly, "that I'm an expert. Yet."

"What the heck are you doing?"

The three of them froze.

"That child shouldn't be riding yet," Jarrod called.

Gil and Colt both stepped forward, preventing the

distraught therapist from getting any closer to Eric. *Good.* Amber was worried he'd startle the horse.

"Excuse me?" Colt was saying.

"Gil, I'm sorry," Jarrod practically snapped. "But—"

"Is everything okay?" Mrs. Peery asked Amber in a worried voice.

"It's fine," she answered as calmly as she could.

"He shouldn't be up there without some basics first," Jarrod was arguing. "That's especially important for children with—" he lowered his voice "—disabilities."

"That child is having fun," Colt said.

"It won't be fun if he falls off," the other man retorted.

"He's not going to fall off."

"Oh, yeah?" Jarrod countered. "And how would you know that, cowboy? You ever work with disabled kids before?"

"No," he said. "But I've grown up on horses. No one's going to fall off a plug like Flash."

Jarrod leaned in, saying very quietly but intensely, "He has no lower leg."

Amber quickly glanced at the Peerys to see if they'd also heard. They had.

Colt's response was equally low and ferocious. "He doesn't need one to ride." The Peerys looked over the horse at each other, clearly confused.

"Okay, that's enough, you two," Gil said. "Amber.

Bring Flash on over here. We'll let Eric finish his ride some other time."

"Yeah, like when *I'm* in charge," Jarrod muttered.

"Jarrod," Gil said quickly.

"You ready to get down?" Colt asked, clearly forcing a smile as he stepped forward.

"Do I have to?" Eric asked.

His mother patted his thigh. "It's time, honey," she said softly.

"You need any help?" asked Mr. Peery.

"Nope," Colt said, moving to Eric's side. "We're good."

But Amber could tell he was furious.

"Come on down, buddy," he said, gently lifting the child off Flash's back.

"Aww, drag," Eric said.

But Eric's mother was beaming. "I've never seen him so excited," she whispered to Amber. Her smile faltered a bit. "After the accident…"

Amber gently touched the woman's arm. "I know. They withdraw into themselves. But something about horses…"

Mrs. Peery watched as her son went up to Flash's head.

"Thanks, horse," he exclaimed, his eyes bright.

"He loves it," she said in a low voice. "I haven't seen him smile like that in…well, a long time."

"His reaction is the reason I'm here," Amber confessed.

Colt was squatting next to the child, showing him

how to touch Flash's nose. The cowboy had calmed down somewhat, but Amber could tell he was still mad as all get-out.

"Actually, it's the second reason I'm here." She turned to Mrs. Peery. "I'm doubling as a speech therapist for the next eight weeks, but I'm interning as a hippotherapist at Camp Cowboy."

"You mean you don't work here permanently?"

"No. I joined up for the first session of the year."

"I was so glad we got in," Eric's mom declared. "We've been trying for six months now."

"Gil—" Amber pointed her chin to where her boss stood "—said if I like doing this, I'm welcome to join them for the session in March." She watched as Gil looked from Colt to Jarrod, who appeared to be arguing.

"I'm hoping we'll be allowed to return in March, too," Mrs. Peery said with a glance at her son. "We were put on a waiting list for this session, and even then they didn't call until after the Christmas break. Just before New Year's." She frowned. "Someone needs to open up a place like this year-round instead of for eight-week sessions."

"I agree." But Amber knew Camp Cowboy operated in eight week segments for a reason. To help more children in need.

"Hippotherapy seems so promising," Mrs. Peery said.

"And Camp Cowboy has some of the best hippo-therapists in the business. I'm hoping they'll give me their insights—you know, teach me how to work with children and horses. Become more than a speech therapist."

Mrs. Peery's eyes were bright. "I think you're going to do *great*."

"I hope so."

"Here," Colt said, reaching for Flash's reins, "I'll take him back to his stall."

Amber hadn't heard him come up, even though she'd had one eye on his argument with Jarrod this whole time. "Can I help?"

"No." She and the Peerys trailed him as he led the horse from the arena.

"He doesn't look happy," Mrs. Peery whispered as they stopped by the gate.

"I think he's mad at Jarrod for telling him he shouldn't have put Eric on Flash."

"Oh, I hope not. Eric loved it so much."

But as she watched Colt head back to the barn, Amber heard Jarrod say to Gil, "He has no business working with special needs kids."

The director nodded.

"He's not trained," Jarrod added.

"I'll talk to him," she heard Gil reply before pasting a bright smile on his face and turning to Eric.

"Did you have fun?"

"Yup."

"Just wait until you get better at it," Gil said.

Colt disappeared with Flash into the barn.

"I hope he doesn't get in trouble," Mrs. Peery murmured.

"Me, too."

Amber wondered if she should follow Colt.

"Oh, the helmet," Mrs. Peery said.

"I'll take it back," she said quickly.

"I can do that," Jarrod offered.

"No, thanks," she snapped.

What a jerk.

But before she could dash after Colt, Mrs. Peery stopped her. "Thank you," she said. Amber noticed the woman had tears in her eyes. "I mean, really, thank you. It was wonderful to see Eric smile again."

One day, she hoped to say the same about her nephew.

"You're welcome." Amber turned away and vowed that, yes, one day she would.

But first she had to see what was up with Colt.

DIRTY ROTTEN BASTARD. He should have clocked the guy in the face. Who did he think he was?

Have you ever worked with disabled children before?

"As if you need a degree to ride," Colt muttered under his breath.

Flash snorted.

"I know," he said. "Pompous ass."

"You okay?"

He turned, stunned to see Amber behind him in the stall.

"Fine," he said curtly.

"Liar."

He just shook his head. Where was Flash's halter? He spotted it in the shavings.

"I'll get that," she said, obviously following his gaze. She handed it to him the proper way—crown piece up.

She was learning.

"Thanks."

"For the record, I think putting Eric on Flash was the right thing to do."

"For the record—" Colt slipped Flash's bridle off, then slid on the halter "—I have more experience with horses than every hippotherapist at this camp combined."

"I know," she said, even though she didn't really know any such thing. She just didn't think now was the time to argue.

"Eric was having a great time until Bozo came along."

"He was." She watched as Colt flipped the stirrup up, hooking it on the saddle horn.

"All you need are your knees to hang on."

"I can attest to that," she said. Her own knees felt chaffed where the saddle had rubbed against them.

"Eric's prosthetic was on his lower leg," Colt said. "I could tell."

She could, too.

He undid the leather strap that attached to a wide rubber piece. The girth, she thought it was called.

But before he could jerk the saddle from Flash's back, she rested a hand on his arm.

"I know Eric was in no danger."

Colt's hands were shaking, she noted in surprise.

"I did *not* put that child in danger."

Was he stricken by guilt? Why did he seem so devastated? So disappointed?

"I know you didn't," she said, gently rubbing his arm. A man's arm. The hard cord of muscle beneath his shirt sent a static charge up her fingers. Or was that from something else?

"I would never intentionally put someone in danger."

"Of course not." She slid her hand up to his shoulder. So hard. So masculine. So tempting to touch.

He shook his head and pulled the saddle off, heading toward the tack room before she could say another word.

She almost leaned against Flash.

Amber crossed her arms in front of her, disgusted with herself. Had she learned nothing from watching her sister fall head over heels for a cowboy? A man like the one who'd just walked away. A man who didn't know the meaning of the word *commitment*.

"I must be losing my mind."

She felt something nudge her leg.

Mac stared up at her.

"Hey, boy." She reached down and stroked his fur.

It took a while before Colt returned, snatching up a brush.

"Um, you want to get a bite to eat after this?" she said, still rubbing Mac. "The cafeteria is open."

"No."

Colt's tone was as impersonal as a doctor's.

"Okay, sure. Yeah. I understand. No problem." She gave Mac one last rub and turned away.

"Amber, wait."

She forced herself to keep walking, Mac following behind her.

"Amber."

She kept moving.

Catching up, Colt blocked her path. "Mac, get back to the barn." His dog glanced first at her, then at him, then reluctantly—or so it seemed—returned the way he had come.

"I'm sorry," Colt said. She watched as he tipped his head back for a moment, releasing a breath. "I didn't mean to snap. I'm just pissed. And…sad."

"Sad?" she asked, forgetting for a moment how prickly he'd been acting.

"For Eric. That kid will have to go through the rest of his life feeling different. And if he doesn't know that now, I'm sure other kids will remind him of it. It upset me." Colt shook his head. "And then the horse whisperer came along and got me angry."

"I've got to go," Amber said, pulling away from him.

"What?" he asked.

"I just remembered I have to do something."

It was one thing to be physically attracted to a man, quite another thing to be attracted to the person he was inside.

Chapter Seven

She didn't see him the rest of the day.

Thank God for that.

Amber didn't want to like Colt. Not when she was so damn attracted to him. That way lay danger.

So she suffered through a restless night. When she finally dragged herself out of bed she told herself not to worry. Yesterday had been a fluke. An aberration. She was over it now.

Still, when he wasn't around at breakfast, she wasn't disappointed, although she did wonder where his dog was.

Two hours after sunrise Camp Cowboy became a bustling hub of activity.

Her nephew arrived today.

Heading back to her room after breakfast, she tugged on a black turtleneck. She'd learned that San Francisco was cold in the morning, far different from Sacramento, where she lived. Once that early morning fog rolled in, the temperature dropped by a good twenty degrees. That meant jeans and a thick pair of socks.

"You ready?" one of her coworkers asked, exiting her room at practically the same moment as Amber.

The woman—one of the live-in volunteers— smiled. Melissa. Long, brown hair. Matching brown eyes. Pretty smile. Friendly. Amber had liked her right off the bat.

"As ready as I'll ever be," she answered.

They walked together down the stairs to where the staff was meeting in the lobby, the area between Gil's office and the cafeteria.

"Thank you, everyone, for coming," said the director, taking center stage in yet another polyester suit, this one gray. "I don't know about you, but I'm excited."

The words stood as a reminder of what Amber had come here to do. Learn. To get over her fear of horses. Help Dee.

"As you all know," Gil added, the light fixture above his head shining on his bald scalp, "the schedule will remain the same every day."

Against her better judgment, she looked around.

And there he was.

In his black jacket and cowboy hat, he was hard to miss...and he was staring right at her.

"Who's *that?*" her neighbor whispered.

"One of the horse wranglers," Amber answered in an aside.

"Well, he can sure wrangle me."

Amber just shook her head. Gil was speaking again.

"The kids will be down at the barn right after breakfast. I expect the kitchen staff to help in this endeavor." He glanced behind him, toward the food prep area. At least ten white-clad people stood behind a glass partition. Amber could smell the eggs and bacon that had been on today's menu.

"Those of you who've been here before know the drill. We'll need a full slate of therapists ready and waiting at the barn every morning to supervise the kids."

Colt was still looking at Amber. She could feel it. But why? Hadn't he gotten the message last night?

"Horse personnel," Gil went on. "Your animals will need to be saddled and ready by 8:00 a.m. You'll need to be on hand at all times. We'll break for lunch at noon."

Amber tuned him out. She'd already seen the schedule Gil was talking about. It'd been in her new-hire packet.

"At one o'clock, we'll resume working with the horses."

Colt didn't appear to be listening, either. At least he wasn't staring at her anymore.

"I'd like to remind everyone," Gil said firmly, "that the children at this camp are our first priority."
Children. Dee.

"Last year," he continued, "we had a few hitches, but this year I expect perfection from everyone, even the new hires. I want this to be the best facility in the nation for challenged children."

Someone began to clap, then another person. Soon the room was filled with applause and whoops of excitement. Amber knew she should be equally inspired, but she was too busy looking around for Colt.

He'd disappeared. And she felt…abandoned. Silly. It wasn't as if they were friends. Or as if she should befriend him at all.

She forced her thoughts elsewhere, because she would be dealing with Colt soon enough. Gil appeared to be wrapping things up.

"All right. The first bus arrives in—" he checked his watch "—any minute now. Go upstairs, grab your jackets or whatever you need to get. Do me proud, people. Above all else, let's help the children."

Those were words she should live by, Amber thought, pushing away from the wall.

"You look sad."

Her heart leaped at the sound of the male voice, but it wasn't Colt who'd spoken. A man she'd never met stood behind her.

"I'm just wishing the weather would change," she said with a smile. "Amber Brooks." She offered her hand.

"Steven Simpson," he said back. Blue eyes and black hair. Cute in a noncowboy, completely normal sort of way.

Why can't you be attracted to him?

"Do you have a brother named Bart?"

He seemed to appreciate her lame attempt at humor. "No, but I have a sister named Jessica."

That made Amber laugh. "Obviously, you've been asked that question before," she said.

"Once or twice."

To her excitement, he turned out to be another of the certified hippotherapists. Thank God. Maybe she wouldn't have to work with Jarrod anymore. She spotted the pompous blond talking to Gil. Not surprising. Probably kissing the camp director's ass.

"You ready for this?" Steven asked.

"I think so," she said.

"I am, too," Melissa exclaimed, leaning into the conversation. The young intern's expression was filled with excitement. "And who's this?"

"Melissa, Steven. Steven, Melissa."

The two of them started talking eagerly, which was okay by Amber because she was abruptly dealing with self-doubt. Wondering if she should have driven up to the Sonoma care facility where Dee had been a resident for the past few years, maybe taken him down to San Francisco herself. But Dee was…difficult. He required round-the-clock attention. She'd found it impossible to take care of him and hold down a full-time job. So she'd done the next best thing. Enrolled him at one of the best facilities in the state of California and then driven in from Sacramento to visit him every weekend. But that had done little good. Her nephew was so disconnected from the world he acted as if she wasn't even there.

Maybe horses would provide the breakthrough

she'd been looking for. Lord knows she'd tried everything else.

She followed the crowd outside. Still no sign of Colt. But a giant diesel pusher that looked almost like a tour bus was headed up the road, its motor growling like a grizzly. Somewhere behind her she heard a rooster crow, but she focused all her attention on the black bus. Like Dee, all the children lived in the area, but he'd been on the bus the longest, since he came from Sonoma. His caretakers had put him on at five this morning. Poor pumpkin was probably tired—not that any staff here would know it.

"Okay," Gil said. "Once the kids are unloaded, we'll take them down to the barn one by one. Tomorrow we'll start doing things in groups, but today I just want the children to see the horses, maybe touch one—nothing more. They won't be riding until next week, so no need to rush things."

Amber found herself wondering if that had been for Colt's benefit. She hoped not.

Where had he gone?

"Those of you not working down at the barn will be responsible for bringing the kids' luggage up to their rooms."

"Oh, man," someone grumbled.

"First ones down to the barn will be Amber and Melissa, with Jarrod as the hippotherapist."

"Right on," Melissa said.

Son of a— Oh, well. Amber would *not* let this spoil her mood.

"The child you two will be working with is Dee." Gil met her gaze, all but giving her a wink at their little secret. "Just speech therapy today, Amber. Don't worry. You won't be riding any horses." He glanced at the crowd. "And while Dee is down at the barn, someone will need to bring his bags up."

"I'll do it," a young woman offered.

"Terrific. Thanks. We'll need all hands on deck today while the kids settle in," the director added, his ring of gray hair nearly the same color as the fog above them. "Have fun, people."

Fun.

That seemed impossible. She'd be dealing with a man who made her heart do funny things and another man she couldn't stand.

And then there was Dee.

She was nervous, she admitted. Keyed up. She did her best to peer through the tinted windows of the bus, but all she saw was the white reflection of the lodge in the shiny surface. She hoped he wasn't fidgety from his long ride. He could become difficult when he wasn't allowed to move around a lot.

The sound of the engine grew louder, the crunch of gravel filling the air. Her heart rate increased every foot it traveled, until at last the bus pulled to a stop in front of them. Amber jumped when the hydraulic brake hissed. All she could make out were dark shapes inside. She knew they had nurses and caretakers on board, too. The vehicle looked packed.

"Here we go," she heard someone say. She glanced back.

Jarrod. Lovely.

The door opened with another gust of hydraulic fluid.

"I had them put Dee in the very front," Gil said, giving her a secret smile.

"Okay, thanks," Amber said, consumed by the urge to hug him for his thoughtfulness.

"You know someone on the bus?" Jarrod asked.

"No," Amber lied. And she didn't feel bad doing it. This was none of his business.

"Well, as lead therapist, I'll go in and get the child."

"Actually," Gil said, "Amber can manage. Down at the barn, you take over."

Jarrod looked confused, maybe even a little perturbed, but he was smart enough not to say a word.

She scooted forward, her heart pounding so hard she would bet people could hear it.

At the door, she smiled at the driver.

And there he was, his dark hair mussed up as usual. Dee's button nose was a little red, probably because he'd been rubbing it, a nervous affectation of his. Surprisingly, however, his big brown eyes were alert. He was clearly intrigued by his surroundings, his head turning to take everything in.

Her heart swelled.

This was why she was here. To help her nephew, and with any luck, other kids just like him.

She wasn't here to kiss cowboys.

Chapter Eight

"Dee," Amber called, hoping he'd look in her direction.

He didn't.

"Did you need my help getting him off the bus?" Melissa asked from behind her. One of the other volunteers brushed past to keep unloading the other kids.

"Sure." Now Melissa's help, she didn't mind.

It was darker inside the bus. The driver, who sat in the front seat, was engrossed in his paperwork.

"Dee," she said again, softer this time. Loud noises upset autistic children, as did touching. She took care not to reach out and startle him.

"It's time to leave the bus."

He knew she was near, knew she wanted his attention. She glanced around at the other children. Some were autistic, like Dee. Some had other afflictions such as Down syndrome. Some were physically handicapped. Most got up without much prompting and followed a camp worker off the bus.

"Dee?" she said again.

And though she'd had years to get used to his condition, it always broke her heart to see him like this. She'd been by her sister's side at his birth, back when Logan had been a nice guy and her sister had been filled with pride. But then it'd all fallen apart. They'd suspected something wasn't right with Dee when he was three. By four he'd been diagnosed. By five Logan was out on the rodeo trail, ostensibly to make more money. But they'd all known the truth. He couldn't stand the sight of his son. And then he'd caused the car crash that had taken her sister's life, and he'd gone to jail.

Everything had happened so fast. One minute Amber had been holding her sister's hand, the next she'd been helping to bury her. And Logan? Well, he was better off out of their lives. Forever.

"We might need to help him up," one of the nurses who'd accompanied the kids said.

"I just hate to do that. He doesn't take to physical contact very well."

"Yeah, but sometimes there's no other way."

She was an older woman with kindly gray eyes, and Amber knew she was right. It was part of the reason she'd put him in a full-time care facility. She'd needed help with him—and hadn't been too proud to admit it.

"All right, let's go."

But before she reached for him, she bent her head close to him and said, "Dee, I'm dying to show you something."

And the nurse, bless her heart, waited patiently, children squeezing past them.

"There are horses outside." Amber dared to move her hand closer to his. "Horses," she said again, louder. "You want to see them?"

Her heart stilled as she gently made contact.

He didn't pull away. Didn't do anything, just continued to stare out the window. She followed his gaze.

He could see the horses.

Colt was down there, grooming Flash, and Dee was transfixed.

"Let's go see," she said, clasping his hand.

He didn't resist. She thanked the good Lord above for that. Of all the types of autism, Dee's was the most severe. She knew that, tried to prepare herself for their visits. Oftentimes, it didn't work.

"Come on," she said, guiding him up.

Did he understand? Sometimes she could swear he did. But as she'd explained to Colt, an autistic child's wiring seemed to be scrambled. Sometimes it worked, sometimes it didn't.

"Nnnn," he said, squinting against the foggy sky. At least that's what it would look like to most laymen, but Amber knew he was squinting because of all the new information his brain was processing. At times it would be too much for him to handle and he would stem, but not today. Thank God, not today.

"Over here," she said.

This was why she hadn't worried someone would

figure out they were aunt and nephew. He acted as if she was a stranger; he'd *always* acted that way.

And it broke her heart.

"I'll walk down with you," Melissa said, bending down near Dee's ear. "Hi, Dee, I'm Melissa."

Jarrod just stood there, arms crossed. He didn't even move forward to meet Dee. What a jerk.

"Come on," Amber said gently.

Each child—thirty of them—would be working in groups with other therapists. Dee was first on the list for this morning. They'd do this for eight weeks. And all the kids had dossiers—diagnosis, prognosis, method of therapy. So Amber knew Melissa wouldn't touch Dee, just as she knew Melissa would follow her lead when it came to dealing with her nephew.

"Here we go," Amber said.

Dee seemed to know where they were headed. Or maybe he was just drawn to the horses. Once again Amber felt herself wondering what it was about the beasts that attracted kids. She could feel her own heart beat just a little faster as they approached.

Or was that because of Colt?

What would he think of her nephew?

She would never know, she reminded herself firmly, because he would never find out who Dee was to her. And yet she wanted to tell him everything. It frightened her how badly she wanted to do that.

Dee, however, seemed impervious to anything

other than the animal in front of the barn. He couldn't take his eyes off Flash.

"Nnnn," he said again, pointing.

"He's nonverbal," Jarrod observed.

"Yup." Amber wondered if Jarrod had read Dee's dossier.

"Horse," she repeated, enunciating the word carefully. It was like double therapy at the camp. She would work with the children's verbal skills while someone like Jarrod worked to make a breakthrough via the horses.

"That's Flash," Amber said, noticing the direction of her nephew's stare. "And that's Colt standing by his head."

Woof.

Amber straightened suddenly.

"What was that?" Jarrod asked. "Sounded like a dog."

From inside the barn came a streak of gray, white and brown. Amber froze. Dee and Melissa did, too. "That's Mac, Colt's dog."

"Dog?" Jarrod said. "He has a *dog* here?"

"Mac!" Colt shouted. "Mac, stop."

The dog ignored him.

"He likes people," Amber said. And he was headed straight for Dee.

"Son of a—" Jarrod jumped in front of Dee. She had to give the therapist credit for reacting so quickly. Dee had never been around dogs before, and who knew how he'd react?

"Mac," she warned. But the dog was on a mission. "Mac, no!"

The animal darted to the left around the adults, his tailless rear end seeming to make him more agile than normal dogs. Amber tensed, knowing her nephew could take this wrong, expecting a shriek of terror as the dog jumped. His scream would be followed by body tremors and then "the crash," as she'd dubbed it over the years.

But Dee giggled.

"Mac," Colt called, coming up behind him. "Gosh darn you, dog."

"Get him off of the child," Jarrod ordered.

"No, wait," Amber said, as Colt moved to do so. "I think Dee likes him."

The boy giggled again, and Colt stepped back.

"I can't believe you let your dog run free," Jarrod snapped.

"He's usually well-behaved," Colt said.

"Obviously not anymore."

"Shh, you two," Amber ordered. "Quiet."

They watched as Mac stretched up, his front paws resting on Dee's chest. The little boy giggled yet again.

"Easy, Mac," Colt told him.

Dog and child had eyes only for each other. The little boy reached down. Mac went still.

Well, that wasn't exactly true. His entire back end swung left and right. If he'd had a tail, it would have been wagging. But his front end? That didn't move.

"Go ahead, Dee," Amber encouraged.

Tentatively, her nephew lowered his hand. When he buried his fingers in the animal's fur, he cooed. Amber knew exactly how he felt. She'd been intrigued by that fur, too.

"Has he ever been around dogs before?" Colt asked softly.

"Not around— I don't think so." *Damn it.* Five minutes in her nephew's company and already she'd almost blown it.

Dee looked around, his brown eyes seeking out and finding hers. He smiled.

"I think he likes you," Colt said.

He recognized her. Amber had wondered if he would. It was one thing to visit a child on weekends in his own home, another to take him out of it and have him recognize you. Sure, she'd known him his entire life, but who knew what went on in his mind?

"I still think you should kennel the dog," Jarrod said.

Amber inhaled deeply. Her eyes burned. He'd smiled! When had she ever seen him do that? Once, maybe? When he'd been younger. Much younger. Back before he'd gone quiet.

"I don't think he needs to be kenneled," said Melissa. "I think having a dog around is a good idea."

"Do you like him?" Amber asked.

"I'll be talking to Gil about this," Jarrod said.

"You do that," Colt retorted.

Amber ignored them.

"He's not upset by the dog," Melissa said.

No. Her nephew seemed completely enchanted by the animal in front of him. Dee's smile turned into more giggles and his hands began to move faster and faster. It was typical autistic behavior. They didn't do things halfway, but all out.

"Easy," Amber said.

But Mac took it all in stride. And when Dee sought her out again, she wanted to cry. That was definitely a smile. It'd been so long…. So damn long.

"If he reacts like this to Mac, I wonder what he'll do around the horses," Melissa said.

"Well," Amber sniffed. "Let's find out. Come on, Mac."

"Maybe you should put the dog away," Jarrod suggested, glancing toward the lodge. A few more kids were headed toward them.

"No," Amber said. "He's fine."

"For now," the therapist snapped.

"If something happens, I'll take full responsibility."

"If you say so."

Colt wanted to throttle the man. Then again, he'd been short-tempered all morning.

All night.

All damn night he'd thought about her.

"Hi," the dark-haired girl said. "I'm Melissa."

"Colt Sheridan," he said, shaking her hand.

"Nice to meet you, Colt. I'm a volunteer here. Anything you need me to do, you just ask."

"Thanks," he said gruffly, glancing back at Amber. Clearly, what had just happened had affected her deeply, just as his own interaction with Eric had touched *him* deeply.

"Dee," she said, "slow down."

The little boy had spotted the horse tied at the front of the barn. It didn't help that Mac seemed to be guiding him toward the animal.

"Don't let him rush up to the horse," Jarrod said.

"It'll be okay." Colt stepped in front of the child nonetheless.

"Don't touch him," Amber warned, but he could tell she didn't mean it harshly. "He doesn't like physical contact."

"Unless it's with a dog." Melissa smiled.

"I don't want him rushing up to the horse," Jarrod repeated. "One wrong move could upset this child seriously."

Who was this clown? He might be a certified therapist, but he had a lot to learn about kids and horses.

"Mac, down," Colt ordered, instantly rewarded by Mac dropping his front paws to the ground. Dee stopped, too.

"Okay, good," Jarrod said, as if he'd orchestrated the whole scenario. "I'm going to take the lead. You all just stand back and watch."

"Uh, don't you think this should be more of a group effort?" Amber asked.

He ignored her. "Hey," he said, squatting next to Dee. "My name's Jarrod and I'm going to introduce you to a friend of mine."

"Don't talk to him like he's an infant," Colt said.

Jarrod's eyes all but stabbed him. "Excuse me?"

"He's a child," Colt said. "He might be a special needs child, but he's still human. He can hear. You're talking to him like he's three years old."

"He is three," Jarrod said. "Mentally."

"Okay, you two." Amber stepped between them. "That's enough. Not in front of this child."

Dee didn't appear to care, but Colt respected Amber's request. Jarrod looked ready to pop a seam.

"Am I running the show or not?" he demanded.

"We *both* are," Amber said. "I respect that you're a hippotherapist. I'm here to learn from you. But I'm a therapist, too. This is a team effort, and if you have a problem with that, I suggest we both talk to Gil."

Jarrod didn't say anything.

"Now," she added.

Colt wanted to clap Amber on the back.

"Fine," Jarrod said. "Amber, bring him on up to the front of the horse and we'll see what happens."

Colt stepped back. "I love this part," Melissa said as the two therapists stood side by side. "It's always so exciting."

He'd gotten a glimpse of that yesterday with Eric, but today wasn't anything like that. Dee refused to get close to Flash. He stopped about three feet away, and didn't even look at the horse. He was fascinated by Mac.

"Would you like to see the horse?" Jarrod asked the boy. He'd lost the preschool voice.

Colt glanced at Amber. She was staring at Dee so intently it appeared she'd forgotten to blink.

"I don't think he wants to move," she said.

"I think you're right," Jarrod replied. "I'll bring the horse to him."

That's what they'd done yesterday. For Eric. Colt had learned, while during research last night, that today would be all about introducing the children to the horses, nothing more. Before each child was allowed to ride, he or she would go through basic instructions on a pommel horse. That wasn't scheduled to happen until next week. According to Gil, Colt's job was to simply lead the horses up to a child and keep an eye on things while the therapists went to work.

"Dee," Jarrod said. Mac stood meekly in front of them. "This is Flash."

Amber had knelt next to the boy, and Colt was transfixed by the way all her energy seemed to be focused on the child.

"Dee," she said. "Flash is a horse." She tipped down so that she interrupted his line of sight. Dee was so intrigued by Mac that he leaned to the right to keep his eyes on the dog.

But Amber was patient. "Dee, I need you to focus on the horse." She moved into his line of sight again.

"Do you want me to put Mac away?" Colt asked.

"Hmm. Maybe." Colt admired the way she devoted her entire self to this. She never looked away from the little boy she was trying to help.

And this was a woman who'd kept a child from his father?

Why? Why would she do such a thing?

"Let's try it," Melissa said. "I'll grab Mac's collar." The intern met Colt's gaze. "Will he mind that?"

"No." He shook his head. "But he'll come if I call him."

"I don't think that's a good idea," Amber said quickly.

"I think it's a *great* idea," Jarrod countered. "The dog's a distraction. No doubt about it." He shot Colt a look that conveyed his disgust.

He's a cattle dog, buddy. He's better with horses than you are.

"He'll move off too fast and that will upset Dee," Amber said. "We need to avoid making sudden movements. Best to do this slowly."

"I say ditch the dog," Jarrod insisted.

"If that's possible." Melissa gently tugged the dog away, her eyes darting between the boy and the animal and another group fast approaching.

"Nnnn," Dee began to moan, his hands beginning to flail.

"It's agitating him," Amber announced.

"Yeah." Melissa released Mac's collar.

"Don't give up *now,*" Jarrod prompted.

"Darn it," Amber said. "I want him to be aware of the horse. That's why he's here."

"He's too in love with Mac," Jarrod said, shooting Colt yet another glare. "You should never have let that dog loose."

"He's part of the team," Colt said firmly. "That dog can herd an animal faster than any human."

"Great, if we ever farm cows he'll be perfect."

"You don't *farm* cows."

"Colt," Amber interjected.

"You might think about putting Mac up next to the horse's head," Colt offered after a moment's pause.

Amber looked up quickly. "Will Mac mind that?"

"He's a ranch dog," Colt explained. "Horses are part of the program."

Amber turned back to the little boy, clearly torn. "I don't know. The last thing we want is a stimming episode."

"No." Melissa's brown eyes widened. "We don't want that."

"Stimming?" Colt asked.

"It's when a child goes into a sort of meltdown," Amber explained.

"It's common with autistic children." Jarrod made a sound as if that was something Colt should know.

Putz.

"But the whole purpose of this initial meeting is

to get him used to horses," Amber added. "So let's put Mac by the horse."

Melissa reached for him again. The gray dog moved willingly enough, but it was clear Dee didn't like it. Colt had never been around a special needs child. Their reactions were just so physical. Dee didn't only moan, it seemed as if every limb went into action. Every single one of his nerve endings.

"Mmmmn," he moaned.

"It's okay, Dee. We're just moving the dog," Amber said. "The *dog*. Can you say *dog?*"

Melissa stopped Mac right in front of the horse. "Can you drop Flash's head down?" she asked.

In response, Colt pulled on the gelding's lead. Mac eyed Flash's big head warily. The dog was used to chasing horses, not sniffing their noses. Colt would swear Australian shepherds had a love-hate relationship with the animals. This was one of those hate moments, but to do Mac credit, he didn't growl or show his teeth. He held still, all the while giving the horse a look that said, *One wrong move, buddy, and you're dead.*

"I don't think your dog likes this very much," Amber commented.

But it was working. Dee stopped moving. They all watched as the little boy looked up.

"Horse," Amber said. "This is a horse, Dee. Can you say horse?"

The horse, as Dee had earlier, had discovered Mac's fur. It buried its muzzle in the hair behind

Mac's collar. The dog shot Flash another look, one that clearly said *not a good idea.*

"Stay," Colt ordered.

Mac glanced over at him, then at Flash again. Flash lipped Mac's fur.

"What a good dog Mac is," Melissa said, amused.

"I know," Amber said. "Poor Mac."

"Poor Mac."

Everyone froze.

Amber stared at the child in disbelief. "He spoke," she said softly.

Melissa stood up. "Aww, Amber," she said. "You're crying."

"I am," she admitted.

And it shocked Colt how much he wanted to pull her into his arms, to comfort her and tell her the real reason he was at Camp Cowboy. Because as he'd watched Amber work with Dee, and as he'd observed Eric the day before, Colt was beginning to wonder if Logan was wrong.

Or had lied to him.

Chapter Nine

Her elation lasted all day.

As Amber let herself into her room that evening she was exhausted yet happy. It helped that working with the rest of the kids had gone equally well. Sure, there were a few less than stellar moments; some of the kids were like Dee, refusing to focus on the horse. But for the most part each child was intrigued by the big animals that had been led before them. Eric, the boy Amber had met the day before, was the biggest star of all. He'd taken to working with horses like a pro.

"Amber?"

It was Colt on the other side of the door.

"You in there?"

She debated whether or not to respond. All day she'd been forced to work with him. To stare at him. He was remarkably gentle with the kids.

She loved men with a soft touch.

She opened the door. "Hi, Colt," she said brightly. Mac was at his feet. During the day, the dog had become Camp Cowboy's unofficial mascot, much to Jarrod's dismay. Everyone loved Colt's dog.

"Mac, no," Colt said when the dog darted into her room.

"It's okay." She opened the door wider. "Do you want to come in?"

He wore his black cowboy hat. Amber wondered if he slept with the thing on. The thought caused her to blush, because she couldn't imagine ever sleeping with him.

Oh, yes, you could.

"I was just wondering if you'd eaten."

"Yup. Had the chocolate mousse for dessert. Yum."

He stepped inside. She watched as he looked around, as if looking for something. As usual, she felt dwarfed by his size. She'd never met a man who made her feel so…so aware of herself and her femininity.

"What's up?" she asked when it became apparent he had something to say.

"Do you have a family member that's autistic?"

She gasped. How did he know? "I, well, I…"

"You do, don't you?"

How to answer? Would he realize Dee was her nephew? Had he already guessed? Had her emotional response to Dee's success that day given her away? Or maybe he'd seen her check in with Nancy on how Dee was settling in.

"Never mind," Colt said. "I can tell by your face that you do."

She gulped. "I don't know what to say."

"Whose child is it?"

"What do you mean?" she hedged.

"Well, obviously it's not your own child."

"What makes you say that?" she asked. "Many special needs children require full-time care. It wouldn't be implausible for me to have a child, one in an assisted living facility somewhere."

"But you don't, do you?"

Really, what would it hurt to tell him the truth?

Except she didn't want him to know.

Dee was her secret. Her sister's son. The nephew she loved. "I don't think that's any of your business."

But to her surprise, Colt didn't look disappointed by her answer. He seemed relieved. She had a moment to consider the strangeness of that reaction before he threw her another curveball.

"You're not at all what I expected. I thought you'd be stuck up. Arrogant."

"Why?"

He seemed flummoxed by her question. "Your vocation," he said. "I thought only stodgy academics had therapy degrees."

Relieved that he'd dropped his interrogation, she laughed. "So all educated therapists are stodgy, huh?"

"I shouldn't be in your room."

"Colt," she said softly. She wasn't laughing anymore.

Because Colt wasn't exactly trying to leave. In fact, he was advancing. "All day, I watched you, thought about you," he murmured. "I can't seem to help myself. I don't like women who value careers over everything else."

"What makes you think I value a career over everything?"

"This," he said, splaying his hands. "The way you've thrown yourself into learning something new—all so you can help children. Or the child in your life who's such an awful lot like Dee."

"I think you should leave now."

"No," he said. "Not until I get to the bottom of this."

He was inches away, so close she could smell him. He didn't wear a cologne. He didn't need to. The man smelled like a potent combination of sweat and pine shavings, and she realized it was a scent that turned her on.

He turned her on.

"I want to know if this will get any better if I kiss you."

"Colt—"

"So I'm—" he slowly reached for her, his eyes almost black beneath his cowboy hat "—going to kiss you."

"I don't think—"

He bent his head and she knew, just *knew* she'd been kidding herself. She could have thrown him out…if she'd wanted to. Trouble was, she didn't want to. And so when his lips connected with hers, she held still. And when his hands drew her closer, she leaned toward him. And when his teeth grazed her lower lip, she sighed.

That sigh was all the invitation he needed.

His tongue touched hers and she moaned.

He plunged deeper. His hands touched her through her shirt, and his tongue withdrew from her mouth, only to thrust back inside again. His big, manly hands made her ache.

He lifted the edge of her shirt from her waistband. She arched to give him better access, and when his fingers found her bare flesh, her skin acted as a conductor of electricity to various parts of her body.

But one part in particular.

An area that warmed and tingled and reminded her that she hadn't had sex in…well…a long, long time.

"Colt," she gasped, coming up for air. "We shouldn't."

"I know." His hands pressed against her abdomen. He was trying to guide her toward her bed.

"We're all wrong for each other."

"I don't care."

You know what? She didn't, either. Then he was kissing her again and she wanted, even if only briefly, to feel that delicious desire that only a man's touch could bring.

"Lie down," he ordered.

She shook her head. They were about to make a huge mistake. Huge.

"Fine." He scooped her up.

"Colt!"

He tossed her onto the bed, and the headboard rattling against the wall. She bounced a few times, the mattress springs squeaking, but then he was on the bed with her.

"Take off your shirt."

"No."

He drew back and lifted the hem.

And for some reason, she found the whole thing amusing. Her first official day on the job and she had a man in her bed and coworkers on the other side of the wall.

She should be ashamed.

"Sit up."

She did.

He tugged her shirt off so quickly she didn't have time to think, and when his hands reached behind her and unsnapped her bra, she instinctively covered herself.

"No, don't." With his big hands he clasped her upper arms and guided her back. "No," he repeated softly. He took a moment to study her before jerking his hat from his head and tossing it onto her dresser.

"You have beautiful breasts."

She didn't. They were too big. And they sagged. They weren't fake and perky and tight like the breasts of rodeo groupies.

"I'm going to kiss them."

Her nipples hardened instantly. She wanted that, wanted his mouth on her. She really did. Her body arched in anticipation again as he leaned toward her. She could feel his hot breath against one of her breasts.

"Hey," someone called out in the hall. A male someone.

The both froze. Had they been found out? If Gil had been told there were two employees in a room together…

"Did you get the health report on the kid in number one?" the guy asked. One of the interns. Or caregivers. Clearly *not* talking to them. Thank God.

"Colt," Amber said, ready to stop this insanity. But he was looking at her, his gaze so heated she couldn't move.

"This is crazy."

"I know," she said.

"I don't care."

"I don't, either."

He kissed her again, hard. Then he was moving down, his tongue finding her nipple again. She closed her eyes and, arching, sighed, "Oh, Colt."

There was a thump on the other side of the wall, but it didn't deter him and in fact seemed to heighten the sexual intensity. The suckling sounds he was making at her breast were erotic. The knowledge that someone might hear them, might figure out what they were up to… She should care about that, she really should. His hand began to move down her bare skin. His fingertips glided toward her belly button, and her stomach muscles contracted. She moaned. His mouth. That wonderful mouth…

He shifted to her other breast, not quite distracting her from what else he was doing.

Unhooking the snap of her jeans.

Her hands found his shoulders. She meant to push him off, to stop him from doing what she knew he was going to do.

Touch her. *There.*

But she lacked the willpower to do more than run her palms up and down his arms, to shift a little so that when he finally did slide his hand toward her center, he had easy access to her—

Her gasp was so loud she was sure her neighbor heard. She tried to bite her lips, but the feel of him suckling her nipple at the same time his hand stroked her soft folds…

"Colt," she said again. "Oh, Colt."

She would lose it if this kept up much longer. She could feel the tremors begin to build, those sweet tremors that she hadn't felt in so, so long and that caused her willpower to fly out the window.

What was wrong with this?

His mouth began to follow the path of his hand.

They were two consenting adults.

His tongue circled her belly button.

There was nothing bad about—

She gasped.

Her orgasm came so quickly, so unexpectedly, that she cried out in shock.

"Shh," he soothed.

"Shit," she muttered as her whole body seemed to burst outward, then contract, then burst all over again.

"Oh, goodness," she moaned. She wanted it to last. Wanted the feeling to go on and on and on.

She barely heard the knock on the door.

"Hey," a man called. "You okay in there?"

Amber's body continued its erotic beat.

"I'm fine," she managed to gasp weakly.

Colt nuzzled her belly.

"Just fine," she called again, softer this time.

God, she was fine.

Chapter Ten

"Was that good?" he asked, admiring the way her hair fanned out on the pillow behind her.

Colt watched as her eyes opened wide. "Yeah. It was good."

He wanted it, too. Wanted to rip open his jeans and plunge inside her. But shit, if that person hadn't just knocked on the door, but come into the room... they'd have been fired for sure. There was a strict "no fraternizing" policy at the camp. Colt had been warned.

"I've got to go," he said, forcing himself up and off her.

"Colt. No. Don't leave."

She wouldn't say that if she knew what he was really doing here. "I need to take Mac for a walk," he offered by way of excuse.

She looked disappointed.

"I'll see you tomorrow." He scooped his hat from the dresser and crammed it on his head.

This had to stop.

This *had* to stop.

Damned if he knew of a way to control it, though.

HE IGNORED HER the rest of the week.

Actually, that turned out to be easy to do. There was a constant stream of children in and out of the barn, and more often than not, he didn't even get to see Amber. Frankly, he'd begun to wonder if she'd ditched the whole horse therapy thing. But then he'd catch a glimpse of her working with one of the hippotherapists on the pommel horse. She was just taking care to have no direct contact with him.

And then Logan called.

And it was just damn good luck that he called when Colt was on his way to lunch. One of his female coworkers waylaid him, saying, "Um, you have a call holding for you from a *prison.*"

"Oh." Colt glanced behind him to make sure Amber wasn't around. "What line?"

"Three," the woman whose name he couldn't remember said.

"I'll take it up in my room."

Colt sprang into action, hoping against hope that Amber didn't find out about this somehow. What if the woman talked? Why hadn't Logan emailed him like he'd asked?

"Logan," he said after snatching the phone.

"What the hell is going on?" his friend cried. "I swear to God, Colt, I can't believe you're doing this to me."

"Wait, wait, wait," he answered. "I haven't done anything. I just asked if your sister-in-law was really as bad as you think."

"And what the hell kind of question is that?" Logan said. "You're supposed to be my friend. That woman stole my child. She's a selfish, arrogant control freak."

Which wasn't the same thing as the nasty child abductor he'd described the last time they'd spoken.

"She's not what I expected," Colt explained.

"You're kidding me. You aren't starting to like her, are you?"

"No," Colt said quickly. "She's just nothing like I expected."

Or you described.

"You crapping out on me?" Logan asked, a portion of his words interrupted by a long beep, followed by the message, "You are speaking to an inmate of the California Correctional Department. Please hang up if you have reached this number in error."

Colt wanted to hang up.

His stomach had congealed into a knot. This wasn't going how he'd expected.

Well, what did you expect?

Did you think Logan would tell you something that would change your mind about Amber?

Lord, Colt wished he would.

"I just think she might have changed," he admitted. "She's not the heartless bitch you described."

"Yes, she is! She won't let me talk to my son. She won't even bring him by for a visit."

Because maybe Logan's son couldn't talk.

Colt sat up suddenly. "How autistic is Rudy?"

"What?" Logan cried. "He's not autistic."

"Are you sure?"

"What the hell makes you ask that?"

"Just answer the question, Logan."

"He's not autistic," his friend said firmly. "Maybe he's a little different. The doctors called it a learning disability. But that's all."

He was lying. Or maybe not lying. Maybe Logan refused to accept the realities of his child's health.

"When was the last time you saw Rudy?"

There was silence, but only for a moment. It was interrupted by another long beep, followed by the warning message. But when Logan answered, Colt could hear the wariness in his voice. "A year ago. And before that, maybe another year. I've seen him maybe four times over five years."

"And what happened?"

"Nothing," he said.

"What happened?" Colt demanded.

Another pause. "The kid freaked out a little bit. So what? Most kids wig out when they see a parent in prison."

So what? After everything Colt had learned about dealing with disabled kids, he had a good idea. Rudy could be autistic. Could be severely autistic.

Was he at Camp Cowboy?

Was it possible? Was one of the kids at the camp Amber's nephew? He immediately thought of Dee.

"Do you have a picture of him?"

"Why?" Logan pounced. "Do you suspect where he might be?"

"I might," Logan admitted.

"Oh, man, Colt, I'd sign over the registration papers of Ronnie tomorrow if you could tell me where Rudy is. Crap. I should have given you a photo before now. The only one I have is from when he was younger."

"Send it anyway."

"You bet I will. Anything to find Rudy."

Why?

Colt had heard Logan might get parole soon. Was that why he wanted to find Rudy? So he could snatch him away from Amber? If it was his son, Colt would want to do the same. But Rudy wasn't...like normal kids. Colt was certain of it.

"Just email me the photo."

"I'll have to scan it in," Logan said. "That means I'll have to wait until I have access to a computer. Give me a few days."

A few days. That meant the weekend. Colt didn't think he could wait that long. But he had to.

"Whatever it takes," he said.

"Thanks, buddy," Logan said. "Thanks a lot."

Colt hung up, collapsing on the bed. There were thirty kids at the camp, half of them autistic. That would make it easy to narrow down.

He might find Rudy today.

And if he did? Then what?

He had no idea.

HE'D BEEN IGNORING HER for a week.

And Amber was hurt, she admitted, staring out her bedroom window.

It was stupid. Ridiculous, really. They were wrong for each other. He obviously thought the same thing. She should be grateful to him.

But she wasn't.

And now it was Saturday morning. The weekend, and even though the kids were in residence 24/7, she had them off, which meant she had nothing to do. And she was feeling sorry for herself.

Someone knocked on the door.

Amber's heart leaped.

"Amber? You in there?"

Melissa. Damn it.

"I'm here."

Melissa let herself in. "Come on," she said excitedly. "Let's go down to the barn."

"What? Why?"

"I just saw a horse trailer head that way," her new friend said. "I think we have some new horses arriving."

"Oh, well, I don't know…" Colt would be down there. Amber didn't think she could stomach seeing him.

"Come on," Melissa urged, grabbing her hand. "You look so glum. This'll be fun."

But as they left the shadow of the lodge, the sun already high enough in the clear blue sky to cast one, Amber told herself this was a mistake.

"Don't you think Colt is cute?" Melissa asked with a smile and a flick of her long brown hair as they walked toward the barn.

"Oh, um. I hadn't thought about it."

"Come on." She punched her in the arm. "You had to have noticed how hot he is."

Yes…yes, she had. "He's not my type."

"Really," Melissa drawled. "He sure is *my* type. Does he have a girlfriend, do you know?"

Yup. Just as Amber had thought. The man could attract women by the dozen. One more reason to stay away from him.

"Oooh, look. There he is," Melissa said.

They'd made it to the barn without Amber even noticing. And Melissa was right. There was a trailer in front, with CAMP COWBOY stenciled on the side, and beneath it, THERAPUTIC RIDING RANCH, SAN FRANCISCO, CALIFORNIA. Colt was standing by the cab and talking to the ranch manager, whom Amber hadn't seen in a good week.

"Hi, Buck," Melissa called out. The grizzled old man in the straw cowboy hat looked over and waved. Mac stopped dancing around and headed straight for Amber.

"Hey, Mac." She stroked his soft fur.

"Hi, Colt," Melissa added.

Amber gave her colleague credit; she didn't gush. But Melissa's interest made her sick.

She wanted Colt.

"Hey," Colt said, his eyes seeking hers.

Amber gave Mac one last pat and walked toward him. "Hey," she answered.

"Have you met Buck?" Colt asked. "He's the ranch manager."

"Yes, of course." Amber shook the old cowboy's worn and work-hardened hand. "Last week. But you've been gone awhile."

Buck nodded, his stooped frame making him appear older than he was. "Out buying more horses." He hooked his fingers into his jeans. He was short and had a portly belly, but she'd heard he was one of the best at managing horses. "Too many kids, not enough rides," the stocky man said with a smile.

"Can I help unload them?" Melissa asked. Mac was begging for attention from her now.

Colt went to the rear of the trailer and opened the door without another word.

He's just doing his job, Amber thought.

Mac caught on to what was going on and raced after him. It amazed her how the dog knew exactly what to do. Mac backed up, his eyes on the trailer, ready to act the instant his human needed help.

"My dad had a rope horse," she heard Melissa say.

"Well, then," Buck said, "you can lead the horse Colt's about to unload to the third stall on the right."

Hooves banged inside the trailer. Mac's head tipped sideways. Amber moved to the right so she could see inside. Was Colt getting trampled? It sure sounded like—

He led a horse out.

Idiot! It was just hooves on the trailer floor. But for a minute she'd felt...she'd felt terrified. Worried about a man she liked.

She liked Colt.

"Give the lead to Melissa there," Buck ordered.

Colt didn't even look at her as he handed over the brown horse. Melissa's smile was wasted, for he simply headed back in.

So it wasn't just her, Amber thought.

"You can lead the next horse."

It took her a moment to realize Buck had spoken to her. "Me?"

"Nobody else standing next to you, is there?"

Amber heard the same banging and thumping as before, only this time Colt led out a spotted pony. "Oh, my gosh, he's adorable."

"It's a she," Colt said.

When she glanced up she found him staring at her in a way that made her heart beat faster and her mouth go dry. It was all she could do to remember to take the lead rope from him.

"Fourth stall on the right," Buck said.

"Okay." Amber took one last glance at Colt. "Come on, girl."

"Petal," Buck said. "The pony's name is Petal."

Despite the fact that she really didn't trust any horse, small or not, "Petal" amused her. "Let's go see your new home."

The little pony followed meekly behind. Mac trailed them as if waiting for a chance to jump in and help. There was something about ponies that kids—and, apparently, adults—couldn't resist. She suspected the camp's autistic charges would be no more immune to their charms than any other child in the world.

"You're going to be such a pampered pony," Amber told Petal as she opened the stall door. Mac appeared to know that he needed to stay outside. She paused for a moment to get her bearings, and noticed that someone—probably Colt—had taken the time to lower the horse feeder and the water inside. "And wait until you meet the kids," Amber added, leading the tiny animal forward. "You're going to love them."

"Oooh, that one is so cute," Melissa said, obviously done putting her horse away. She peered at them from near the doorway. "Look at those spots. It's like a mini-leopard appy."

"A miniature leopard what?"

"Appy," Melissa said. "An Appaloosa. They're the horses with spots. Not a big fan of them myself. They can be as stubborn as mules. And I've never been big on white around the eye. But this girl is adorable. Look at her big brown eyes." Melissa came in and wrapped her arms around the pony's neck. "She's just so tiny."

"She's going to be real good for the kids," Buck interjected. Behind him, Colt walked past with yet another horse in tow. "Picked her up for a song," Buck added. "Came from a carnival outfit down south. She was one of those pony ride horses. Bet she'll be happy not to have to walk in circles a million times a day."

"No kidding," Melissa said with a sympathetic shake of her head. "Poor thing. I've often wondered what kind of life that was for a pony. Tied up all day. But no more. Now you get to have kids love on you all day long."

"Anything else you need me to do?" Colt asked.

"Nope. That's the last. Just keep an eye on them tonight. Make sure they settle in good."

"I'd like to go riding," Melissa said. "If it's okay, Buck."

"'Course it's okay," the older cowboy said. "I would encourage all you therapists to ride."

He looked straight at Amber.

"Oh, um, I've got some stuff to do up at the lodge," she mumbled.

"Nonsense. That can wait. Colt, go and saddle up Flash for her."

"No, really," she said. "I have reports to write. Parents to call. I don't have time to ride. I'd just like to pet the pony for a little bit longer, if that's okay. She's more my size."

She couldn't look at Colt. Was worried that if she met his gaze he'd see how much she'd missed him all week. How every time she saw him she remembered what they'd done in her room.

"Suit yourself," Buck said. "Melissa, I take it you know how to saddle a horse?"

"Sure do."

Amber felt a pang of envy toward her friend.

"Great. You can take Flash then. I'll saddle up one of the other horses. I understand you can ride all the way to the beach from here. Let's see if that's true. Colt, why don't you park the truck and trailer out back for me and then keep on mucking stalls."

Amber focused on the pony. She wanted Colt to stay behind. To talk to her.

She heard a noise. Her heart leaped.

"You okay?" she heard him ask.

"Fine."

"You don't look fine."

He started to enter the stall, ordering Mac to stay outside.

"Colt…"

"Shh." He closed the door. "Just shh."

He touched her face. And Amber was lost.

Chapter Eleven

What are you doing?

He shouldn't touch her. What if Logan really understood this woman better than he did? After all, Colt had met her just a few days ago. But he couldn't seem to stop himself.

"Just shh," he warned her, glancing outside the stall to make sure they were alone.

Logan would skin him alive if he knew of the lascivious thoughts Colt was having about his ex-sister-in-law. And yet he couldn't seem to pull away.

He kissed her. He didn't care that Buck and Melissa were outside. Didn't care that Amber and he were in the middle of a stall. Didn't care about anything.

He could fall in love with this woman.

The thought came as a shock. He drew back.

"What's wrong?"

God, what a mess.

Logan was wrong about her, Colt was certain. Amber didn't keep his son away out of cruelty. She did it for Rudy's sake.

Colt had the little boy's picture in his pocket, had been checking it against the children in the camp ever since he'd received it last night. But Logan was right. It was too old. The child in the picture was too young, his face softened by baby fat. The kids at this camp were older. Colt had sent Logan an email advising him of the fact, but he had yet to hear back.

"Colt?"

He drew her toward him, so conflicted, so filled with longing. She was so incredibly lovely. "Amber," he said softly.

The moment their mouths connected, he couldn't seem to stop himself. His tongue slid across her lips and he tipped his head to the side for better access. He fitted his body to hers in such a way that she couldn't misunderstand his intentions.

"Colt," she moaned when he nibbled the shell of her ear. He felt her shift, and she captured his hand.

Brought it to her breast.

"Touch me," he heard her whisper. "Touch me *here*."

She pressed herself against him, then did some exploring of her own.

"Jeez," he murmured when she touched him, stroked his length.

She didn't let the fabric of his jeans deter her. He dropped his hand, his mouth finding the side of her neck. And then *he* found *her* center.

"Yes." She moaned again.

Their lips met once more and he almost lost himself. Here. In the middle of a damn stall.

"Amber," he murmured.

"Just grab the curb bit."

Buck. They sprang apart.

"They're all hanging on the wall to the left," the ranch manager was saying.

As she passed, Melissa glanced in the stall, saw them and stumbled.

"And this is the horse's fetlock," Colt pronounced loudly.

"Uh-huh," Amber said.

But Melissa wasn't stupid.

She gave them a look and kept on walking.

"Crap," Amber said, straightening. "Crap, crap, crap."

"Amber—"

She left him standing there, nearly colliding with Buck on her way out.

"Excuse me," she said, and then was gone.

Mac tried to follow, but Colt ordered him to stay.

"What happened?" Buck asked.

"Nothing," he said blandly.

It was a lie.

Chapter Twelve

"Damn it, damn it, damn it," Amber cursed as she closed her bedroom door behind her. She stripped off her clothes.

She smelled like Colt.

"There must be something wrong with me," she muttered.

Her room was on the utilitarian side, with off-white walls, white drapes at the window, a single bed against one of the walls. Wooden chair, a tiny desk, tiny closet… She sank into the chair.

Someone knocked on her door.

Colt?

"Amber, you have a phone call," one of her co-workers called. "Line two."

Not Colt. Disappointment sluiced through her.

"Hello?"

"Where's my son?"

"Logan," she said sharply.

"Why the hell haven't you returned my emails?"

She took a deep breath. "Logan, I can't put him on the phone. He can't talk to you. You know that."

"Because you won't *let* him talk to me."

She clenched the phone. "He's autistic."

"So he's got a learning disability," Logan said. "That's nothing."

Lord, she was tired of his denials. "I *have* tried, countless times, to put him on the phone. He won't do it. Something about the plastic against his face—"

"Liar."

"I'm going to hang up."

"Don't you dare."

This was how it always went. Logan would insult her. She would lose patience trying to explain things. He would call her a bitch, or worse. She would hang up.

She took another deep breath. Not this time. Time to take the bull by the horns. To settle the matter, because quite frankly, she couldn't take this anymore.

"Okay, look," she said. "I promise to arrange a visit next month." She could take Dee back to Sonoma herself, pop in to see Logan on the way there.

"Liar."

"Stop saying that! I'm not lying, Logan. I'll call the prison and arrange it right away."

"Why don't I believe you? Oh, wait, I know. Because then you would have done it before this. It's been more than a year."

She sighed. She didn't understand the animosity. She was doing the best she could with Dee. *She* was the one who'd been wronged. It was *her* sister who'd died. She should be the one yelling at him on the phone. For driving drunk.

"I promise, Logan," she finally said. "I'll set it all up next week."

She hung up before he could call her a liar again. But she sat there for a long time afterward, staring out the window. She could see the barn from her room, and occasionally Colt and Mac down there.

She got up to go visit Dee.

He was staying in a room on the next floor down. Someone had come up with the idea of painting the hall blue, with a rainbow snaking around the doorways and walls. At the end of the rainbow closest to the stairs was the nurse's station. The head nurse, Nancy, smiled and waved. Amber had invented a cover story to explain her visits. She'd let it slip that Dee was the subject of a paper she was writing for her master's thesis. Nobody had questioned her.

She found him in his room, staring outside, ironically, just as she had been.

"Hey, kiddo."

He didn't turn. Didn't look at her. Didn't acknowledge her presence in any way, shape or form.

"How do you like your bedroom?"

As if he would answer. She almost laughed at herself. She sat on his bed. Like at his regular care facility, Dee was pretty much left to himself here. He was supervised, of course, but was usually in his room unless it was time for one of his therapy sessions, or mealtime.

Amber wondered what that was like. Wondered what he thought of all of it. But she had a feeling he preferred to be left alone. Autistic children were the epitome of antisocial.

"I think I'm going to take you to go see your dad in a few weeks."

He blinked, sunlight softening the edges of his face.

"I really don't want to, but I think it's time to try again."

Dee didn't seem to care. He was starting to look like a young man, she noticed. Even his hair had darkened.

Where had the time gone?

Her eyes watered, and she wondered if she'd done the right thing in keeping him away from his dad. Should she have given up her job, too? Gone on social welfare? Kept him with her? Or had it been the right choice to move him into a place that specialized in giving the care he needed? That kept him safe and away from things that might harm him? She honestly didn't know.

And she felt so alone.

She stood to see what he was staring at. He was looking toward the barn. Of course he was. His room faced the same direction as hers. She tried to spot Colt, but all she saw was Mac.

"Dog."

"What's that, sweetie?" she said, leaning toward him, wishing she could hug him.

Sis, I'm trying so hard.

But Sharron couldn't hear her. Neither could Dee, it seemed. The boy touched the window, his finger-tips leaving smudgy circles on the glass.

"Dog," he said again.

Amber froze, then closed her eyes against more tears. She lifted a hand, wanting to touch him.

"His name is Mac," she said, gently resting a palm on his shoulder. Dee didn't move away. "And you're right, he's a dog."

"Dog."

"Mac," she enunciated.

"Dog," he said again.

She'd take it. At least he remembered dog. And it was a minor breakthrough. A word. His second in ages. Something more to build from.

She had no one to tell. No one to share the victory with.

"Maybe Colt will bring Mac by to see you later."

Dee didn't say anything.

"I'll ask him if you want."

He continued to stare toward the barn. And that was okay with Amber. There were so few moments like these. As he grew older, there would be even less. It would be just Dee and her. Although not if she allowed Logan back in their lives.... One day, she would have to give Dee up—at least part of the time. Logan would want him back, she'd begun to accept that. Even if Logan had pushed his child away at the onset of Dee's autism, escaping to the rodeo. He seemed to have come to terms with it....

She spotted Colt and pressed her hand against the glass, too, amusing herself for a moment by covering up his hat with her thumb.

"He's different," she said softly.

A rodeo cowboy. What irony.

She made a decision then, one that she knew in her heart was right. She was so weary. Sick of being alone.

"I love you, kiddo," she told her nephew.

She turned away, heading toward...well...she didn't know what she was heading toward.

But she wanted to find out.

HE NEEDED TO GET off his ass, Colt thought, sweeping the floor more furiously. Needed to do a better job trying to match the photo in his pocket to the kids at the camp. To keep his mind off Amber.

"Hey there."

He almost dropped the broom.

"You look busy," she said.

"Hey." He forced himself to meet her gaze.

Her blond hair was illuminated by the light behind her, the edges burnished gold. When he was younger he'd pictured his ideal woman. Amber was it. But that had been a long time ago, back before his life had fallen apart.

"You doing anything right now?" she said softly.

"Why? You need something?"

It seemed she might not answer, but then she squared her shoulders, looked him right in the eye. "I was hoping you'd take me for a ride," she said. "Next week's kind of crazy for me. I should get some time in the saddle before all hell breaks loose."

You want to find Rudy, don't you?

"Flash?" he asked.

"Uh, sure," she said, glancing toward the gelding's stall.

"You could always ride Petal."

"Aren't I too big for her?" she asked.

He felt his lips twitch. "I was kidding."

"Oh. Well, then, I guess I better go catch Flash."

"I can do it for you."

"No, I'll do it," she said, turning away. His dog tried to follow in her wake.

"Mac," he called.

The Australian shepherd obeyed his command, but Colt could tell he didn't want to. He'd taken a shine to Amber. Colt didn't blame him.

She picked up the halter, studying it for a moment. Flash was eating his dinner in a corner of his stall, his ears swiveling back and forth.

"This won't upset his stomach or anything, will it?" she asked.

"What?"

"Interrupting his meal."

"No." Colt stared at her from beneath the brim of his hat. "Horses in the wild are frequently startled by prey. They can graze for hours and then run for ten miles without any harm coming to them."

She slid the stall door open. He was pleased to see she held the halter the correct way this time, and that she walked right up to Flash. Since the horse was eating, it paid her hardly any attention. In a matter of minutes she'd buckled the headpiece and then stood back, proud of herself.

Colt couldn't help but smile. "Good job."

She tugged the horse away from his food. Flash wasn't exactly thrilled to have his dinner interrupted, but he followed her out. Colt hung back at a distance as she walked toward the front of the barn. It wouldn't be dark for a couple hours yet, but the eucalyptus trees shielded the barn from the sun. He had a feeling the people who'd built this place had planned it that way. Amber didn't seem to notice the waning light. She marched right up to the hitching post, wrapped the lead rope around it and executed a perfect slipknot.

"Wow," he said, pleased on her behalf. "Impressive."

"Thanks." She eyed the horse. "If only I didn't feel like jumping out of my skin."

"You'll get used to him."

But she frowned, her expression doubtful.

"Let me go get my horse," he added.

"Your horse?" she asked. "You have one here?"

He would if he played his cards right. The thought depressed him.

"No. Not my own. I meant one of the camp's horses. Oreo," he said. "Big paint."

"Paint?"

"It's a color," he explained. "And a breed. Here, I'll get him. You can start grooming if you want. Just grab one of the buckets out of the tack room. You know what you're doing now. I'll be back in a minute."

"Okay," she said warily. "But if you hear a scream, call 911."

What was it about her that could make him smile one minute and want to avoid her the next? He tried to reason that out as he haltered Oreo, Mac by his side again. By the time Colt tied the horse next to Flash he was still no closer to figuring her out.

"I'll saddle up if you brush Oreo," he offered.

He could see her relief. "Deal."

Mac hung back as he made short work of the task. Colt was looking forward to this.

Aside from today, it'd been a week since he'd spent any time with her. A whole week and not once had he gotten up the courage to go to her room… either to see her or to snoop around.

"You ready?" He led his saddled horse toward hers.

"I think so," she said, brushing back a strand of hair being tossed by a breeze. He smelled the pungent scent of the eucalyptus leaves and then her own unique smell. Sugar cookies, he thought.

"Use the mounting block," he suggested, pointing. They'd been schooling the kids on it all week.

"Wow," she said. "I wish I could have used that before."

"Better for you to learn how to pull yourself up," he said, wheeling Oreo around with a tweak of the reins while she positioned Flash to mount. "You never know when you might have to dismount out on the trail."

"Is it dangerous?" she said, wide-eyed.

"No, no. Sometimes you need to open gates and whatnot. Or I might need you to hold my horse. No big deal."

Mac followed them at a distance. Colt almost told the dog to stay behind, but the Australian shepherd needed a good run.

"This isn't working," he heard her say.

He glanced back. She stood on the plastic steps, contemplating the distance between herself and Flash. The horse had stepped away from her.

"Smart-ass," he said.

"Who, me?" she asked.

"No, Flash. He knows what you want him to do. He just doesn't want to do it."

He swung a leg over the front of Oreo and leaped down. "Jump off and reposition him."

She did as instructed, but Flash decided he didn't want to move. "You really are a smart-ass," she told the horse.

"Here. Hold mine."

Flash seemed to recognize authority when he saw it because he instantly did as asked.

Colt motioned for Amber to bring Oreo closer. "Climb aboard," he said, taking the reins from her.

But even with him holding Flash's reins, the gelding sidestepped again, and Amber, who'd chosen that moment to mount, ended up off balance.

"Grab the horn," Colt warned.

Too late. She teetered near the edge of the steps and he knew he would have to break her fall.

"Damn it," he muttered, lunging for her.

But he missed and she slipped off the steps and landed on her rear with a thud.

"Are you okay?" He tugged on Flash's reins to get his attention.

"I'm fine," she said, her brow wrinkling as she winced. "The only thing wounded is my pride."

He felt something strange then, something that took him a moment to identify.

Affection.

He *liked* this woman…*a lot*.

And given that he would soon betray her, that scared the living crap out of him.

Chapter Thirteen

She felt like an idiot.

Amber sat in the dirt, staring up at Colt. He must surely think her a dumb blonde. She couldn't even get on a damn horse.

Instead he appeared as if he wanted to console her. It filled her with warmth.

"Maybe this isn't meant to be," she said in resignation. "Maybe I should just stick to speech therapy."

"Nope," he said quickly. "Best thing to do is get back on the horse."

"I never actually got *on* the darn thing," she said. Mac sniffed at her, as if to offer sympathy. "Can you have a little talk with Flash?" she asked the pooch. "I don't think he understands I'm a beginner."

"Oh, he knows," Colt said. "That's why he's doing what he can get away with." He offered her a hand. She slid her fingers into his, so big compared to hers. She felt diminutive next to him.

Feminine.

She felt like a woman. And it was a feeling she discovered she really liked.

"Thanks," she said softly.

He let her go, but it seemed like he did it reluctantly. "Okay," he said, taking a deep breath. "Try it again."

She eyed the horse, her heart beating so loudly local seismographs likely picked up a reading.

"Hold still, Flash," she said as Colt brought the horse alongside the mounting block. "Mac, make him stay still."

Then she jumped on board so fast Flash didn't have time to pull away.

"Ha!" Her cheeks hurt, she was grinning so widely. "I did it."

"Yes, you did." Colt's brown eyes looked black beneath the brim of his hat. He turned away without a backward glance, swinging up on his horse like Jesse James fleeing the OK Corral. "Follow me."

She told the horse to go. Flash didn't.

"He's doing it again," she stated.

"Push him forward with your legs like you did the other day."

It worked.

Flash moved forward reluctantly, but at least he moved. He tossed his head as Colt led them toward the arena.

"What about Mac?" she asked.

"He'll come along."

Colt was getting farther ahead.

"Are you going to give me a lesson?" she called out. That would make her feel better.

"No."

No? "Then…where are we going?"

"On a trail."

"How do you know there's a trail out here?" she asked as they walked past the arena.

"Buck told me," he said. "It's all public land. If you ride long enough, you can get to the beach."

"I remember. I was there." The thought of riding near the ocean filled her with grim determination. It was something she'd always wanted to do despite not knowing anything about horses. Who hadn't seen beach resort brochures with a couple riding bareback among the waves? Sounded good to her.

At least in theory.

"How long will it take to get there?" she asked.

"Where?"

"The beach?"

He glanced back at her. "We don't have time. This'll just be a short ride."

"Oh," Amber said, disappointed. Maybe one day.

They rode along in silence, Amber marveling that in a few hours the fog would roll in and the entire peninsula would be shrouded in mist. She could feel the early warning of the weather change in the cold breeze that had begun to blow. It made her wonder if she shouldn't have grabbed a jacket. Mac didn't seem fazed. As they passed the arena, the dog ran toward a thick stand of trees that she'd been curious about—tall pines with low-lying scrub beneath. A path led right toward them.

"Hard to believe we're only a few miles from Fisherman's Wharf."

"It's more than a few miles," Colt replied, although it was hard to hear him because he was so far ahead of her. He'd already made it to the trees, and didn't seem inclined to turn around.

She debated trying to catch up to him, but had no idea how to put Flash into second gear. But maybe it was better this way. Maybe she should just hang back and enjoy the ride.

Heh. Enjoy. Yeah, right.

"Colt," she called, when she saw no sign of him slowing down.

Reluctantly, he pulled back on the reins. "What's up?"

She caught up to him. "Nothing."

His eyes had narrowed. "You're doing fine."

"Thanks," she said. Against a backdrop of pines and Douglas fir, he looked like something off a poster. It was still sunny out, but beneath the trees it was chilly. The earth smelled moist and rich. And *he* smelled wonderful. The combination of Colt and trees and the out-of-doors smelled…heavenly.

As they set off again, Mac wormed his way through the brush. He was panting now, his pink tongue hanging out. They entered a denser grove of trees, the tall pines closing in on them.

Amber was enjoying the rocking motion of her horse, just as her autistic charges would once they learned to ride, she decided. Something about it seemed to soothe her frazzled nerves.

"I am one with the horse."

"Good," Colt said curtly.

"But I think it'll be a while before I'm as comfortable around horses as you."

A long, *long* time.

He didn't reply.

"How long have you been riding, anyway?"

His hands twitched on the reins. "How about this," he said as they moved even deeper into the trees. "I tell you something about me and you tell me something about you."

She contemplated the idea. "Okay."

"Who in your family is autistic?"

"Excuse me? Why do you keep asking me that?"

He pulled his horse up so they were side by side. "Your passion for what you do comes from somewhere. I would bet it has to do with a family member."

She shook her head, but in the end, she supposed it wouldn't hurt if he knew.

"It's my nephew," she admitted.

"You have a nephew?"

She nodded. "I do."

"How old is he?"

"Your turn," she said instead. "Where did you grow up?"

He clearly didn't like the question, or maybe it

was the game they were playing. But it had been his idea. "New Mexico."

That took her by surprise. For some reason she'd expected him to say Texas or Oklahoma or some other place known for cowboys with Southern accents.

"Your turn." His horse tossed its head. "How badly autistic is he?"

She gulped. It was hard not to come right out and tell him it was Dee. "Pretty bad." She smiled through the pain it caused her to admit that. "I didn't know they raised cattle in New Mexico."

"Some of the biggest cattle ranches in the world border the Texas and New Mexico state line. Is your nephew the reason you became a therapist?"

"Hey, I didn't get to ask my question."

"You asked me about raising cattle."

"I was merely thinking out loud."

He gave her a look.

"Honestly."

"Fine. Ask a question."

She resisted the urge to roll her eyes. "Do you have any family?"

"No."

It took a moment for his response to sink in. "Not even a cousin or an aunt?"

"No," he said. "And that's two questions."

"Nobody?" she pressed.

"Three," he said. "And no. Not a mom, dad, grandparent or uncle."

She clutched the reins tighter, completely blown away. She'd had it in her head that he came from a big family. That he'd grown up on a ranch. Surely that meant lots of cousins.

Apparently not.

He was staring at her oddly, as if he wasn't certain what to make of her reaction. The only sound for a moment was the dog's panting. Colt kicked his horse forward. Flash kept in step with him.

"My turn," he said. "Do *you* have any family?"

"Yes." But her mind was still chewing on what he'd revealed. What would it be like to have nobody in the world? She at least had Dee. That was something.

"Where does your nephew live?"

Right now, with me.

"Wherever he gets the best care," she answered evasively.

"I meant what town?"

"That's three questions," she said. "Why do you want to know, anyway? And he lives up north."

"Just curious. And that's not a town."

"Near Sonoma," she said.

He leaned back in the saddle. "Sonoma. That's up north?"

"Is that a question?" she asked. "Because if it is, you're back up to three."

"No." His eyes searched hers, as if he wanted to ask her something else, but wasn't quite sure how to pose the question.

"And now it's my turn," she said, echoing his words from earlier. "How did your family die?"

It was a horrible thing to ask. Invasive. Rude. And *way* too personal, and yet she had to know.

But he wasn't going to answer. His expression had turned to stone, his eyes to slate.

"Ask your next question," he muttered.

The trees were starting to thin out. In between them, Amber spotting what looked to be apartment buildings or maybe homes. And was that the roar of the ocean in the distance? Or was that a freeway?

The path they were riding, shielded by trees and lined by shrubs, was beautiful.

"Was it an accident?"

He pulled up his horse again. "It's none of your business."

It wasn't. She knew that. "You asked me about my nephew. That was none of *your* business, but I answered."

"That's different."

She spotted something big and red to her left and stiffened. "Look!"

He didn't move.

"Over there," she added, "through the trees. It's the Golden Gate Bridge!"

She pushed her horse forward, proud of herself for making Flash walk past Colt's horse. Sure enough, the trees opened up farther ahead and a small clearing afforded her a more direct view of the bridge. It was in the distance, but not so far away that she couldn't hear the sound of cars traveling over it—that was the noise she'd heard.

"Check it out," she said when Colt came up beside her. "Isn't that amazing? We're so far away, and yet you can hear the cars."

"Neat."

He said it so harshly, she asked, "What is the matter with you?"

He didn't answer.

"Look, I know it was none of my business to ask about your family, but I thought it might help to talk about it. I'm a therapist. It's what I do. Push people to their limits."

"You're a speech pathologist," he said.

"Ooh, you've been paying attention," she teased, trying to draw a smile out of him.

"And I'm a cowboy," he said. "Me and therapists don't mix."

"That's not what it felt like the other day. Or should we both go back to ignoring the elephant in the room?"

"I'd rather ride." He kicked his horse forward and whistled for Mac.

"We can't ignore what's between us," she called out. As she'd sat there, watching him try to hide how he felt, something inside her had clicked. It all made sense. *This* was why she was attracted to him. What it was that drew her attention.

They were alike.

She'd lost everyone near and dear to her, too.

Well, except for Dee. But her loss was still a fresh wound. She missed her sister terribly. They'd been everything to each other since their parents died in a commuter train accident years and years ago. They'd spent their early lives in and out of foster homes, and it had been terrible. Amber was a therapist because of that, too. She'd seen the effect having no family could have on children, the speech impediments it could cause. So she'd put herself through college. A year after she'd graduated, her sister had died and Logan had gone to prison. She'd been caring for her eight-year-old nephew ever since. For four years now...

She shook her head.

Colt missed his family. She missed her sister. They weren't much different, after all.

Chapter Fourteen

Colt and Mac kept ahead of Amber for the rest of the ride—close enough to keep an eye on her, far enough away that she couldn't ask any more probing questions.

Such as how his family had died.

That he wouldn't think about. Didn't *ever* want to think about.

It hurt too damn much.

The trail circled through the trees, and he pulled up when he spied an even better view of the bridge.

"It's so pretty," she called out.

It was. As golden as the name implied.

The sun had dipped even lower, making it feel like dusk in the forest. So when they emerged from the trees, it was almost a shock to see the sun still above them.

"How'd that happen?" Colt heard Amber call. "We're almost right back where we started."

He took off his hat, tilted his head back and absorbed the sun on his face. It felt good. He wished he could sit here all day. But there was too much to do. And Amber...

She wouldn't leave him alone.

When they got to the barn, Colt jumped down. "Use the mounting block to dismount," he ordered.

"Oh," she said. "You *can* speak."

He grabbed Oreo's halter, made quick work of slipping off his bridle and sliding the nylon harness on.

"Holy moly!" Amber cried.

He jerked around.

She was already off her horse. "I don't think I'll be able to walk for days."

"Damn it, Amber. I thought you'd fallen off."

"Surprisingly, no," she said with a smile. "Apparently Flash doesn't mind standing still while someone gets off."

Colt went back to work.

You're being an ass.

He was. He knew it. But he just wanted to get this over with. To get the horses unsaddled and Amber up to the lodge. That way he could have some privacy. Some time to figure out what the hell was wrong with him, because despite narrowing down where her nephew lived, Colt felt no elation.

"Can I help you take the saddle off?" she asked, after tying Flash.

"No."

When he glanced over at her as he pulled the saddle off Oreo's back, he saw the hurt in her eyes.

"I'll go hang up the bridle," she said.

"No need." He held out his free hand. "I'll take it."

"Colt…"

He grabbed the bridle from her even as he chastised himself for being so harsh. "See you up at the house."

"Uh, okay."

He didn't hang around to see if she had gone or not. After he tossed the heavy saddle on the rack, he rested his palms on the seat. Mac whined, his head tipped to the side, ears pricked.

"Crap," Colt muttered.

He had to get hold of himself. He'd scored a major victory in finding Logan's son. He knew where Rudy was.

How did your family die?

Colt closed his eyes as he thought back to that day, to the site of the accident…the broken railing. The branches near the base of the hill. The gouges in the asphalt.

"Colt."

Pulled from his memories, he straightened with a jerk, and spun around, planning to lash out at Amber. But he didn't have the heart. It wasn't her fault his memories caused so much pain.

He hadn't had a heart since his teens.

"What happened to you?" she asked gently.

He shook his head. "It's nothing." He drew a

breath, then another. "I thought you went back to the lodge."

"I couldn't leave you like this."

"Like what?"

"Upset."

"I'm not upset," he lied.

She took a step closer. "This is about your parents, isn't it?"

"Don't you have something to do?" he asked, tempted to leave.

But she'd already closed the distance between them. Already lifted a hand and touched his cheek. "I've taken far too many psychology classes not to know when someone's lying."

Did she know his whole existence was a lie? That he had no business being here? That the day his parents and his little sister had died, he should have been with them?

"Colt," she said. "You shouldn't keep this bottled inside. It's eating you up."

"You don't know anything about me," he snapped. "Nothing at all."

"I don't," she agreed. "Despite what's happened between us, I don't know hardly anything about you."

Her eyes drew him in. He swore they could swallow his pain. How lucky the children were who had her on their side. How lucky Rudy was.

"Maybe it's better that way," he said, backing away.

But she followed him. "Keeping things inside is never better for you," she said softly.

She moved around him and somehow wedged herself between the saddle on the rack and his body.

"Sometimes, Colt," she said, her blue eyes as big as the compassion in her heart, "you need to let things out before life can get better."

He wanted to turn away. But her eyes held him.

For the first time ever, he found himself on the verge of making a confession. Of telling her what had happened all those years ago.

But he didn't deserve her pity...or her compassion.

"I need to go," he said, brushing past her.

This time she didn't follow him.

SHE DIDN'T SEE HIM for the rest of the day. Not at breakfast, either. It was Monday, and today would be the first time the children would actually ride the horses. A crowd of about twenty or so volunteers, physical therapists and interns—like herself—headed toward the barn.

"I'm freezing," Melissa said with an audible shudder.

"Me, too," Amber said, trying to spot Colt. He must be in the barn.

"Is the sun ever out in the morning here?" her friend asked.

It had dawned another foggy and overcast day, but the humidity made it seem particularly cold. "I don't know." Amber tried to draw further into her jacket, like a turtle.

Buck came out of the barn leading a horse, but so far no Colt. And no Mac, either.

Where were they?

She needed to apologize. To tell Colt she was sorry for pushing. She'd been born too pushy, and that was what made her a damn good speech therapist. She didn't give up. Didn't mind the repetition. She pushed her patients to get it right. Colt wasn't a patient.

"Okay, here's how it'll work," Jarrod said. "We'll break into four teams, each led by a hippotherapist. That means Jackie, Sam and Sarah will be in charge. Whatever they tell you guys to do, you do it. I'll run the other team."

"Who died and made him king of the universe?" Melissa said in an aside.

Amber smiled. "I think the horse-therapist experts need to take control at this point, don't you?"

She tried to avoid the man whenever possible, but the few times she'd bumped into Jarrod at the lodge he'd seemed just as bossy and, frankly, annoying. He'd asked her out last week. She'd said no. Amber hoped that would be the end of it.

"Melissa and Amber, you'll be on my team," he said.

"Oh, great," Melissa muttered.

"We'll need a fourth," Jarrod announced. "Any volunteers?"

An older woman with thick-framed glasses lifted her hand. Maybe Jarrod wouldn't hit on someone clearly over forty.

"Thanks," he said. "Jackie, Sam and Sarah, you want to pick your teams?"

Melissa stepped closer. "Is it just me, or is Jarrod really, really annoying?"

Drops of moisture were clinging to her friend's dark hair. Amber had no doubt the humidity was doing the same to hers. "Really, really, really annoying." She looked past her, to see Colt leading a horse out of the barn, Mac following behind. But the cowboy didn't look up.

Something inside Amber withered.

"The children are on their way down," Jarrod called out. "Let's get it together, guys. My team will go first. Any idea when you'll get the rest of the horses saddled?" Jarrod asked Colt, his tone on the verge of rude.

"They're tacked up in their stalls," Colt said. "Just let me know when you need the next one."

Hah, Amber wanted to say.

"Amber!" someone called. "Can I speak to you?"

She turned, startled to find Gil escorting the three children they'd be working with. Wait a minute... *three?* "Where's Dee?"

"He didn't want to leave his room," Gil explained. "We tried everything. We were thinking of just leaving him be. He could work with one of the physical therapists today, and then later, with you for speech, if that's okay."

Amber glanced to where Mac stood beside the horse.

"Actually," she mused, "I have an idea."

She turned back to her boss. Did he have an endless supply of polyester suits? He looked out of place among everyone else in their jeans and thick jackets. "I'd like to try a little experiment with Colt's dog."

A frown creased Gil's forehead above his glasses. "How so?"

"I think Camp Cowboy's focus should be expanded." When his expression grew even more puzzled, she added, "I think we should use *all* types of animals for therapy."

His eyes widened. "Colt's dog?"

"If Colt doesn't mind. I'm curious if my neph—" She caught herself. "If Dee will respond to Colt's dog. Honestly, it's been tough to get Dee to look at a horse. Mac, however—"

Gil had begun to nod. "Hmm. It's not something we ever considered."

"It's worth a shot," she said. "You can't tell me every child responds to horses."

"They don't," the program director agreed. "And it's always a disappointment. Colt?" Gil called when he came back out, leading a second horse. "We have a proposition for you."

Amber noticed that the moisture had turned Colt's black hat even darker.

"What's up?" He still wouldn't look at her.

"Amber here would like to borrow your dog, if that's okay."

Finally, their gazes connected. "What for?"

She pasted a smile on her face. It killed her to see him like this. Obviously, he was upset about yesterday. "I'd like to introduce him to the other children."

Colt glanced at Mac, then back at her. "I don't mind."

Gil clapped him on the upper arm. "Excellent. I suspect Amber might be on to something, especially after how Dee responded to the dog earlier." Her boss met her gaze. "But are you certain you don't want to wait until later? When you're done working with the children and horses?"

"I have weeks to work with the horses, Gil." Amber smiled. "Mac!"

The dog instantly turned. Amber decided she wanted a pet just like him one day. She loved the way Mac came running, tailless rear end wagging, tongue lolling, eyes shining. She wished his owner would be as happy to see her.

"Come on, Mac," she said. "Let's go up to the lodge."

She wondered if he'd follow her or if he'd want to stay with his master, but the canine didn't hesitate.

"Thanks, Colt," Amber said.

He held her gaze for a split second longer than before. "You're welcome."

And off she went, with Mac at her side. That gave her some comfort. At least his dog liked her.

And Mac loved children.

That became obvious the moment she hit the children's wing and found Eric standing in the long hallway there. He must have been on his way to one of his therapy sessions but paused in delight when he spotted her canine companion. Mac seemed just as happy to see Eric as he was every other child on the floor. They soon attracted a crowd of children. Nancy, the head nurse, tried to keep things under control. But it was a challenge. Amber squatted down at Mac's level, trying to shield him from small probing hands. You never knew what a special needs child might do. Some were like Dee, autistic and uncommunicative. Some had minds that just didn't work right, symptomatic of causes as varied as Down, fetal alcohol or genetic syndromes.

"Okay, guys," Amber called at last. "Time for us to go."

There were choruses of "Aww," from kids and adults alike. Amber smiled.

Yup. A dog was just what this place needed.

She straightened and headed toward Dee's room.

"Knock, knock," she said.

He was standing in the corner of his room, in the space between his bed and a closet. Just standing there. Examining the wood frame around the closet door as if fascinated by the way it connected to the wall. And maybe he was fascinated.

"Hey, buddy, I brought you a friend."

The dog looked around, sniffing, taking in the new surroundings. And then he spotted the little boy. It was funny, but Amber could swear the dog wanted to rush to him. Yet he didn't.

Mac didn't jump up on Dee. Didn't bump into him. Just stood there, waiting to be noticed. And when Dee didn't move, Mac touched the boy's hand with his nose.

Dee turned and looked down.

"Dog."

Amber was so delighted, her mouth dropped open. He remembered!

"That's right," she said, pleased that he remembered. "Dog."

That was the thing with autistic children. You could never be certain what they would retain. Heck, with Dee, they'd never been certain he was absorbing *anything.* Off in his own world. He fed himself, for the most part, but only vegetables that were a certain color. And only if items on his plate didn't touch. And never meat. Dee couldn't stand meat.

Mac backed up a few steps. And to her surprise, Dee followed. Amber squatted down, encouraging Colt's dog to come to her.

"Come pet him, Dee," she urged.

She didn't expect him to comply. Honestly, there was a good chance he really didn't understand her, that he was just following the dog, but Amber didn't care. As long as he responded.

"Sit, Mac," she instructed.

From this angle, she could see her nephew's eyes, and as always happened, the loss of her sister came back in a wave of sorrow. He had her eyes. Who was she kidding? He had her entire face.

"Put your hand out," she told him softly. But her nephew's beautiful brown eyes were fixed on the dog. Amber held her breath as she reached for his hand.

He didn't pull away.

"Pet him," she said, burying his fingers in Mac's soft fur. The dog, bless his heart, held still, staring up at the boy.

"Remember, his name is Mac," she said. "He's an Australian shepherd." She showed her nephew how to stroke the dog. "Isn't he pretty?"

"Dog."

Amber smiled. "Yes, dog."

Mac swung around, poised to move, but waiting.

Amber sat back and watched. "He wants you to follow him," she said, although she had no idea where the dog was going. "Follow him, Dee."

And he did. Mac's rear end began to swing, his blue eyes wide. Tongue hanging out, ears pricked forward, he crouched and then lunged away. The dog was playing with Dee.

But Dee had never played with a dog before. He seemed confused about what to do.

He was engaged, however. Engaged!

Forget the horses. This dog seemed to be all the therapy Dee needed.

"He wants you to chase him," Amber said, going to sit in a chair in the opposite corner of the room.

Mac yapped, then darted toward the boy, only to quickly move away again. With a leap that would have done Superman proud, he jumped onto the bed.

Dee giggled.

He'd laughed.

"Oh, no," Amber said, springing out of the chair as Mac attacked the pillow on the bed. She lunged, but the dog got away from her, pillow in mouth.

"Mac, no!"

Dee giggled again.

Amber paused, turned back to her nephew. "You like that?"

The dog tossed the pillow in the air—or tried. Amber made a grab for it, but Mac snatched it away.

"Mac!"

Dee laughed, a sound so full of delight it brought tears to Amber's eyes.

"Oh, Dee," she said softly.

She'd never, ever, heard him laugh or seen him smile like that. Joyfully.

Mac tossed the pillow in the air again. Amber caught the motion out of the corner of her eye. Quick as a cat, she grabbed a corner, laughing herself when she outsmarted the dog.

"Got it."

Mac didn't let go, though, and jerked it back.

Amber held on, and while Dee continued to laugh, she continued to pull. And then the most miraculous thing of all occurred: Dee reached for the pillow, grabbed a corner.

And actively participated.

Oh, dear Lord.

Amber wanted to sob in joy. Instead, she tugged on the pillow. Mac held on and so did Dee, and Amber laughed until she felt tears roll down her cheeks.

When she heard the sound of ripping, she instantly released the pillow. But not Dee and Mac. Oh, no, the two of them continued with their tug-of-war.

The pillow spewed an eruption of feathers that would have done Vesuvius proud.

"No…!" Bits of down flew everywhere—the bed, the floor, the windowsill to her right.

"Ooop." Dee held the empty pillowcase in his hands.

"Yes, Dee," Amber said, on the verge of laughter again. "Oops. Nancy is going to kill us."

"No," a masculine voice said. "But she'll probably make you clean it up."

Amber wasn't the least bit embarrassed to see Colt. She was glad he could witness this happy moment.

"Gil told me it was okay to come lend you a hand, since all the kids at the barn are riding right now with their therapy teams."

"I didn't do it," she declared, palms up.

She could see the evidence of contained mirth on his face. Spotted the telltale signs. Knew that he had a hard time fighting laughter.

Mac shook himself, sending feathers flying.

"What in the world?" Nancy cried, standing in the doorway.

Amber giggled.

Dee said, "Dog."

Mac barked.

And Colt...well, Colt finally gave in. He laughed, too.

Chapter Fifteen

"You know you're going to need to clean that up," Nancy said, hands on her hips. She peered at them from Dee's bedroom door.

Colt wanted to laugh at the nurse's expression.

"I know," Amber said.

"We'll take care of it," Colt interjected.

He'd come up here under the pretext of lending her a hand, when in reality he'd been curious about which child she'd gone to visit. But he should have known it would be Dee. She was always with Dee.

Her nephew.

He was certain of it. Dee. Rudy. The names were so similar he felt like a fool for not realizing it sooner.

He struggled to mask the grief this realization caused him. Yes, grief. He would have to call Logan. That meant betraying her, and he didn't want to do that.

He closed his eyes.

She wasn't a conniving witch. She didn't hate men. She was a brilliant, beautiful woman who put everyone else's needs before hers.

"You okay?" Amber asked.

"Uh, yeah, I'm fine." He forced himself to look at her.

Dee, her nephew, the little boy Amber cared so much about, was standing next to Mac, his left hand stroking and stroking and stroking Mac's gray fur.

"We haven't been able to reach him before this," she said softly, following Colt's gaze.

"Why not?" He needed to know about this child she tried so hard to protect from the world. Even from his father.

"He's severely autistic," she explained. "He talks on occasion, but only to repeat something he's heard. Echolalia—that's what it's called. A bit of dialogue, something he's mimicking, but never actually conversing with anyone. Today he called Mac a dog, for the second time. He knew what the word was and used it in the right context. That's remarkable."

"So there's hope," Colt said. That's what she was doing here. To find hope for her nephew.

A child Logan wanted to take away from her. A child Logan said had minor social issues. Was his friend consciously misleading him or did he really not understand the extent of his son's condition?

"As long as he keeps responding," she said. "I'm hoping once he gets to ride he'll open up further. Vestibular stimulation has done remarkable things for some autistic children." She looked back at Dee. "There have been a few cases where the child has been cured." She tipped her head. "Well, as cured as possible."

"And if you can cure one child, you might be able to cure others."

Children like her nephew. Children who didn't have someone like her to look out for them.

"Yes. This facility is a model for future camps. The foundation that started it invested hundreds of thousands of dollars, all in the hope of proving this can work. So more children can find the help they need."

"Like Dee," Colt said.

"Yes, like Dee."

He would have to talk to Logan, convince him Amber deserved to be involved in Dee's life. Because no matter what she might have told herself, Logan would soon be out of jail. It seemed incredible to believe. Colt's friend had been convicted of vehicular manslaughter with gross negligence. He'd been sentenced to six years in prison, which meant he had two more years to serve. But with California prisons as overcrowded as they were, there was a shot—a really good shot—he'd be released early. Colt suspected that's why Logan was so determined to find his son. And Amber would be blindsided.

Amber. The woman who loved her nephew so much she would change careers for him.

"Do they always do that?" Colt asked.

She didn't need any explanation. "The stroking? Yes. It's part of their condition. Mac soothes him. I suspect there's a connection between special needs children and animals. All animals. I want to introduce Mac to some other kids next. Study what happens."

Colt wanted her to succeed. He hadn't come to Camp Cowboy looking for a cause, but he'd found one. He'd have to be inhuman not to be affected by what Amber was trying to do for children.

She was a remarkable woman.

"I'm sorry about yesterday," he found himself saying, although maybe he was apologizing for something else.

Her eyes dimmed. It was like watching someone pull down blinds. "That's okay."

"I was a jerk."

"And I was nosy," she admitted.

She looked so pretty. The sun had dipped behind the trees, but light still poured into the room, and into her eyes.

"Friends?" he said.

No. Not friends. He couldn't be her friend. Not with what he knew.

"Friends." She smiled.

It was hell, especially when she held out her hand and he took it, knowing that no matter how badly he wanted to keep on holding it, he couldn't.

He released her. "I better get going."

"You'll want to take Mac."

"No," he said. "Leave him here. Keep on doing what you're doing. See if he helps."

"Will he stay?"

"If I tell him to."

She startled Colt by stretching on tiptoe and kissing his cheek. "Thanks. I'm going to sit with Dee for a while and see if I can't coax more words out of him."

God, she was killing him. Colt knew in that instant that Logan had lied. She wasn't the horrible person he'd made her out to be.

She wasn't horrible at all.

HE HAD A HARD TIME sleeping that night. When he woke up in the wee hours, he told himself to get up. He needed to send Logan an email through his cell phone. It was hard to figure out what to say, though.

Dear Logan. I quit.

That was certainly tempting. But Colt knew Logan would just find some other way to locate his son. And if he did that, Colt wouldn't know about it and then Amber would still be blindsided when Logan came for Dee.

Damn it.

Colt sat at the tiny table in his room, opened up the internet on his cell phone, then loaded his email. He was half hoping there was a message in there. Something from Logan, telling him he was off the hook. Of course, that meant losing out on Logan's horse. But that was okay.

No letter.
It was up to him to make contact.
Logan, he typed, using the tiny keys.

I've located Rudy.

It wouldn't hurt to tell him that, he thought.

He's somewhere near Santa Rosa.

That was close enough to Sonoma to be true, yet not an exact location.

But before I tell you exactly where, promise that you won't cut Amber out of Rudy's life when you get out of jail. That you'll continue to let her see him.

He thought hard over what to say next.

I've gotten to know Amber. She's not the evil person you think she is. She has Rudy's best interests at heart. She loves him. Please don't break her heart.

And what if Logan rejected his plea?
Colt ran his hands over his face. He honestly didn't know.

Begging you, Logan. Give her a chance.

He pressed Send before he could change his mind.

How long he sat there, he didn't know. At some point he crawled into bed. Mac woke him early in the morning by jumping onto the bed and curling up near his feet. Colt tossed and turned from that point on. When he finally got out of bed, he told himself he should be relieved that at least he'd done something to help Amber out.

He wasn't. If anything, he was even more confused. What would he do if Logan demanded to know where his son was? What if he told Colt to get lost? What if…what if…

Colt got up filled with anxiety. And when he caught sight of Amber walking toward the barn later that morning, her blond hair pulled back, blue jeans hugging her body, he felt dread on top of his anxiety. But maybe she wouldn't spot him standing inside the stall.

"Mac, stay," he ordered, because the dog noticed Dee at the entrance to the barn. Colt shook his head. He didn't know what it was about the boy that drew the dog's devotion, but it had been love at first sight.

Love.

He could never love a woman like Amber. He went back to tacking up the horses for the day's riding classes. They were opposites, from two different worlds—his filled with road trips and rodeos, hers with research and self-sacrifice. And then there was his past. Messed up, that's what he was. He knew it. Had figured out long ago why he avoided relation-ships like the plague.

He was afraid.

Afraid of losing something else he loved.

"You done?" Buck asked as he left the neighbor-ing stall.

"Yup." Colt gave a girth one last tug.

"Okay, then. Let's lead the horses on out. We'll do the same thing as yesterday. Bring them one at a time, help the therapists get their charges mounted."

"Got it."

One at a time.

He should focus on the job at hand. Keep his mind off Amber.

"Hi," Amber said brightly.

He was in the stall, untying Oreo.

"Hey," he replied.

"I got Dee down here this morning."

"Oh, yeah? I'm surprised Mac hasn't run off to greet him."

Colt looked down. His dog was facing the door of the barn, his whole body tensed.

"Stay," Colt ordered.

"We might need Mac if this doesn't go as planned."

She was nervous. He could tell by the way her eyes darted over the horse. How she kept glancing back toward the group of people gathering outside.

"Relax," he said. "If this doesn't work, I promise to lend a hand."

His dog had started to whine.

"All right, fine," Colt said to him. "Go on. Say hello."

Mac needed no further urging. Like the herding dog he was, he ran full-tilt toward his human friend, to be greeted by Dee's cry of "Dog."

"You're right," Amber said. "I shouldn't worry. Things will work themselves out."

He ached for her.

There was no other way to describe how he felt. He ached with compassion for all she was going through. He also ached for the pressure of her body against his. To hold her. To kiss her.

"Let's get the show on the road," Jarrod called.

Colt led Oreo forward. His heart beat faster not just because of Amber, but because he, too, was anxious to see how Dee reacted.

"You better be good," he told the horse.

The little boy with the sunny smile was busy stroking Mac again.

"Oog," he said. "Oog, oog, oog."

His obvious delight caused those around them to smile. And if Mac could talk, Colt had no doubt he'd be saying, "Dee, Dee, Dee," in a rhythm that matched the beat of his back end.

"Okay, since this is his first time, let's not give him a chance to balk. Let's lead the horse right on over to the mounting block," Jarrod said. "We'll put him up straight away."

"Do you think he's ready?" Amber said. "He's only ever petted a horse before now."

"You'll never know until you try."

Colt wasn't so sure, but that might have been more to do with disliking Jarrod than his own instincts. He could read body language pretty well, and he would swear that came from working with horses. Dee was engrossed in Mac, but there was something about the child's stance that had seemed to change when Oreo was led out of the barn. He might not have glanced at the horse, but he was aware.

"How do we do this?" Amber asked.

"The same way we did the pommel horse," Jarrod answered.

Colt had watched them last week. Kids had been taught to walk up the wide steps of the mounting block and then get on. Still, this was a whole other ball of wax.

"Lead him on over," Jarrod said.

Buck stood watching from the entrance of the barn, Colt noticed, the cowboy squinting his rheumy blue eyes. Someone placed a helmet on Dee, though it was obvious he wasn't happy about it. He kept trying to tug the thing off. Fortunately, Mac distracted him. Before too long they had the child at the wooden steps. He didn't want to climb those, either, but once again Mac came to the rescue. Colt warily led Oreo up to the mounting block, but Dee had eyes only for Mac. He wasn't the least bit interested in the horse.

"Okay," Jarrod said. "Everyone take up your positions."

Colt had seen this before, too. There would be two therapists on each side. The other four, including Amber, would stand by Dee's legs—two on each side…if they got him in the saddle.

"Okay, Dee," Amber coaxed, and Colt marveled that he hadn't noticed the resemblance before. They had the same profile. "Time to climb on board—just like we practiced on the pommel horse the other day."

Dee kept stroking the dog, a lock of brown hair covering one eye, the white-and-gray-striped shirt he wore nearly the same color as Mac's fur.

"Go ahead and get up there next to him," Jarrod said impatiently.

Amber nodded, climbed the steps of the mounting block and tentatively laid her hands on Dee. Colt knew that was because of the boy's acute sensitivity. She was careful when she nudged him toward the horse, too.

"Nnnn," Dee groaned, his eyes still on Mac.

"Come on, kiddo. This'll be fun. Don't you want to ride the horse?"

"Nnn," Dee said.

"Just try for me, okay?"

But Dee would have none of it. Colt watched from in front of Oreo as the child's body language grew more and more pronounced, all but screaming, *Leave me alone.*

"Just slip one foot in the stirrup."

"Amber—" Colt warned.

"No, no," Jarrod said. "Keep going with him."

Colt shook his head. The guy might be trained to work with kids and horses, but he didn't know squat about reading body language.

"I'm not so sure this is a good idea," Colt said.

"I'm not so sure, either," Amber agreed.

"Do as I tell you and we won't have a problem."

Colt almost walked away. One thing held him there. Amber.

"Okay, Dee," Amber said softly. "I'm going to grab your hand."

Colt tensed. Amber reached for the boy.

All hell broke loose.

A sound unlike anything Colt had ever heard before erupted from the child's mouth. Dee flung himself from the mounting block. The therapists reached for him. Amber cried, "No!"

"Aaaahhhhh!" Dee lifted his head and banged it back down repeatedly, his legs thrashing, arms punching.

"Dee, calm down." Amber had followed him to the ground. "Calm down," she soothed over and over again. Colt's heart broke on her behalf. "Please, calm down."

But there was no getting through to the child. He rolled around on the ground, kicking and screaming and moaning and making noises unlike any Colt had heard before.

"He's stimming," Jarrod pronounced—as if he hadn't had a hand in causing it.

"I know." Colt thought Amber might smack him.

Nobody could do anything about Dee. That was clear by the looks on their faces. They were forced to stand back and watch.

It was Mac that came to the rescue.

He plopped himself down right next to Dee, his eyes clearly fixed on the child's.

Dee stopped moving.

Mac didn't move, either.

"That's incredible," Colt heard Melissa say softly.

How long they stayed that way, he wasn't sure. But then slowly, tentatively, Dee reached out. Mac nuzzled the boy, who laughed.

There were audible sighs of relief all around.

"I don't know where you got that dog, but I want one just like him," Melissa said.

"Me, too." Amber gave Colt a smile.

She could have one all the time if she wanted to, Colt thought. But then he chastised himself. As if they could ever have a future together, with all that he'd kept from her.

"Where'd you get him?" Melissa asked.

"Down south."

"I want that breeder's number."

"Let's get back to work, people," Jarrod said, glancing at his team. "We need to get him up on that horse."

"But…" Amber glanced at Colt helplessly.

"Let Mac help out."

"What do you mean?" she asked.

"Watch." He whistled. The dog instantly came to his side, and Dee sat up.

"Up, Mac," he ordered, pointing to Oreo.

"You're going to put him up on the horse?" Jarrod asked. "That's ridiculous. No dog will do that."

"He's done it before," Colt said, biting back what he *really* wanted to say.

Just be quiet, jerk-wad.

"Sometimes when we're out gathering cattle," Colt added, "I'll give Mac a ride back to the ranch." Granted, he'd always held the dog in his lap, but Mac probably wouldn't care. As it turned out, the Australian shepherd didn't. All Colt had to do was point to the saddle and the dog jumped up. Dee followed right on his heels. Oreo seemed to take it all in stride.

"Go on," Amber said. "Climb on board. Mac wants you to go for a ride."

Did the child understand? Amber had told him that autistic children understood far more than it might appear. For years psychologists had labeled them mentally retarded or developmentally slow. But, in fact, autistic children could have genius IQs.

Dee slipped into the saddle as if he'd been doing it all his life.

"I'll be damned," Jarrod said, clearly incredulous.

Of course, it took some twisting and turning before dog and child settled into the saddle together.

"I wish I had a camera," Melissa said.

Colt did, too. But the sight was something he'd never forget.

"Here." Jarrod held out his hand for the lead. "I'll take over."

Colt almost told him to get lost. But Jarrod was right. Colt was there to tend to the horses; it was the therapist's job to work with the children.

He handed the lead over.

"Ladies, take up your positions, please," Jarrod said.

"Be careful with my dog."

"Thanks, Colt," Amber said softly, glancing up at her nephew as they started the horse walking.

Colt watched them from a distance even though he should've gone back into the barn to lead the next horse out.

"Cluck, Dee," Amber said. "Like this." She made a clucking sound.

They walked away from the mounting block and toward the arena. Mac sat in front of the child as if he were the King of Pasha. And if someone had bet Colt six months ago that he'd be watching a child ride around while his dog sat shotgun, he'd have laughed all the way to the bank. He smiled as the pair coasted along.

"You done good," Buck said, coming up next to him.

"Thanks."

From a distance, Colt heard Amber say, "Do you

see the trees, Dee? Trees." She pointed. Ever the
speech therapist.

Dee's little body swayed back and forth. He began
to smile.

"Look at that," Buck said. "That's what makes it
all worth it."

Dee let go of Mac, threw his arms up in the air.

"Dee ride," he said as clear as a bell.

Colt saw Amber stumble. He heard Melissa's gasp.
Saw Jarrod glance around in self-satisfaction.

"And *that's* why we force them up," Jarrod said.

"Pompous ass," Colt muttered.

"He's like a bull with one horn," Buck drawled.
"Swaggerin' around like he's something special with
his lopsided head, when every cow in the pen can
see he's just a bull with one horn."

Colt felt himself smile. "I'm surprised you put up
with it."

Buck hooked his thumbs in the front of his jeans.
"Well, son, I'd put up with a lot to watch what just
happened over and over again." His rheumy eyes met
Colt's. "I don't do this because of the money, that's
for sure. Though it pays better than most ranching
jobs, and you get a comfy bed to sleep in." He cocked
his head. "But what are you doing here, Colt?"

Spying.

He would have thought that after a week his guilt
would have faded. "It's a job," he admitted.

"Humph. I think you'll find it's a lot more than
that."

Colt knew he was right. He'd already seen that. During the days he'd been at Camp Cowboy he'd watched numerous kids come out of their shells. He'd heard more than a few first words. He'd seen the delight of therapists and children alike, and though he never figured himself to be the soft type, he couldn't deny he'd been moved. Was even discovering a side of himself he hadn't known existed.

"Is it always like this?" he asked.

"You mean chaotic? Rewarding? Loud?"

"That's it."

"You'll get used to it," Buck said. "And you'll find the trouble is worth the price of admission." He winked. "Especially when you have a pretty little distraction in the mix."

Colt followed the man's gaze. Amber was laughing. Dee was smiling. Colt knew in that instant that he didn't want to let her go. For the first time in his life he felt more than mere attraction for a woman.

For the first time in a long time he was tempted to care about somebody besides himself.

Chapter Sixteen

Amber couldn't keep the smile from her face.

He'd used words. In the right context. At the correct moment. A *third* time!

"Did you have a good day?" Gil asked as she entered the lodge. She was tired, but looking forward to catching up with Dee's various therapists to see how the rest of his day went.

"Yeah," she said, pausing by the office door. "It was *great*."

She'd learned a lot. Dee hadn't been the only one to have a stellar time. Other children had been equally affected by the horses they'd ridden. Amber wished she could figure out why. Guess she'd have to crack the therapy textbooks Jarrod lent her.

"Look, Amber," Gil said, "Dee's father called again."

Her stomach dropped.

"I told him you were working and that you'd phone him back."

"Thanks."

"You really think we should add dogs to our therapy program?"

"I do," she said, remembering Mac up in the saddle.

"Okay, then." Gil's wire-rimmed glasses caught the light. "I'll look into it."

"Let me know if I can help." She moved away from the door, lost in her thoughts, and nearly collided with Jarrod.

"You want to get a bite to eat?" the cocky blond asked.

Only if someone gave her a lobotomy beforehand.

"Actually—"

"She'll be with me tonight," Colt said, coming up behind her, Mac on his heels.

Jarrod glanced from one to the other in sudden understanding. "I see."

And when Amber's eyes met Colt's, she saw, too.

"Whatever," Jarrod muttered, turning away.

They were left standing there, together, in the main hall.

"Sooo," Amber drawled. "What's up?"

"I was wondering if you had a moment to talk," Colt drawled right back, in his Texan twang.

In my bedroom?

She almost asked out loud, but didn't have the courage.

"What about?" she said, although just the memory of what he'd done with her when they'd been in her bed together…

She wished he'd do that again.

"I hope you don't mind what I said to Jarrod." He hesitated.

Her heart fluttered like an anxious bird. Seeing him in his black hat and jeans, she was reminded of his innate masculinity, which never failed to excite her. Even now. Standing in a busy hallway, the two were forced to move out of the way as another therapist entered the lodge.

"I don't mind," she said. And then she swallowed back her bout of nerves. "If you meant it."

He looked away for a moment, took a deep breath.... He was nervous.

"I did," he said at last. And then he placed a hand on her lower arm. A big hand, the same hand that'd touched her intimately not so long ago. "There's something about you, Amber. I can't seem to get you out of my mind. I've tried." He rubbed his hand over his face. "Lord, how I've tried. But I can't."

"I know how you feel," she said.

"But there's something I need to tell you—"

"Amber!" Melissa raced down the steps, sounding out of breath. "Thank God. Nancy needs to see you right away. She's in Dee's room."

"Dee?" Amber repeated.

"Yes. Go."

The look in Melissa's eyes scared the hell out of Amber.

She took the stairs two at a time, not looking to see if Colt followed.

She knew the moment she hit the second floor landing that something major had happened. A group of people, including Nancy, stood outside Dee's room, staring in.

"What is it? What happened?" she asked the head nurse.

"Amber," Nancy said, turning toward her, "there's a problem with Dee, and when I looked at the emergency contact information, it listed *you*."

"What's wrong?" Amber pushed her way to the door. Her nephew lay on the floor, his body racked by convulsions.

"Dee," she cried, rushing to him.

"No, Amber, stay back." Nancy grabbed her by the arm. "I know you want to go in there, but you need to keep away. I've got an ambulance coming. We need to keep the room clear for when the paramedics arrives."

Stay back? Not on her life.

"Let. Me. Go." She wrenched free and darted to Dee's side.

"Why are you listed as his emergency contact? Do you know his parents?"

"He's my nephew," Amber replied.

"Your what?" Nancy was clearly taken aback.

But Amber was too busy cradling Dee to care. She stared into his unfocused eyes. The world grew unfocused. Blurry. She felt dizzy. The room began to spin....

"Dee," she murmured, holding his head as tremors

continued to rack his body. "It's auntie," she soothed. "Settle down."

"He can't hear you," Nancy said. "He's seizing."

"No kidding." Amber held him tightly. "Dee, it's me. Calm down, pumpkin. Don't fight it—"

Mac barked.

"Get the dog out of here," Nancy snapped. "I'm sorry, Colt, but he'll have to go."

"I'm not going anywhere, and neither is my dog."

Mac whined, raced to his friend.

And the convulsions stopped.

Dee's back settled onto the floor. His head stopped thrashing. His limbs still twitched, but it was as if someone had turned the power off.

"Oh, Dee," Amber said softly, tears trailing down her cheek. "That's it. Calm down."

Mac moved in even closer. Nancy, thankfully, didn't say a word. The other nurse, a male one Amber had met once before, took Dee's pulse.

"Coming through," someone said a moment later. Amber had been so fixated on Dee she hadn't even heard the sirens. "Everybody give us some space," one of the paramedics, a dark-haired man, ordered.

"I'm not budging," Amber said firmly. "I'm his aunt."

"Right." The guy set his medical kit down next to them. "Then give us some space to work."

Amber scooted back. She didn't know when Colt had knelt next to her. When he'd wrapped his arms around her. All she knew was that when she felt his comforting presence, all she wanted to do was cry. But she couldn't. She had to hold it together. For Dee's sake.

"Has this ever happened before?" one of the fire-fighters who'd arrived with the paramedics asked the room at large.

"No," Amber answered. Her voice hitched. "This is the first time."

She watched as the dark-haired man shone a light in Dee's eyes. Her nephew looked so pale beneath the beam's white light. So small and fragile.

"Dee," she murmured.

Colt's arms tightened around her. He was cradling her from behind, supporting her, and she was grateful for that. If he hadn't been in the room with her, she'd have collapsed in a heap, crying.

"Pupils normal," the man said to his companion, a woman, Amber finally noticed.

"Pulse 90 over 145," said the woman. A blonde.

"Let's get him on the board and out of here."

The blonde nodded, and the pair worked quickly to get Dee immobilized. While they did, another team arrived, from the ambulance company.

"Is he being transported?"

"Yup," said the male paramedic. "But he's stable."

Amber nearly collapsed. Only Colt's arms kept her upright.

"Is there room in the ambulance?" Colt asked as they lifted the child.

"Yeah, sure," a gray-haired man said. "You family?"

"She's his aunt," Colt stated.

"Works for me," he said. "I can get some info from you while we're on the way."

Things moved quickly from there. Colt asked if someone could watch Mac. Melissa volunteered. They got Dee down the steps and into the ambulance in a matter of minutes, Amber keeping a wary eye on him the whole way. One of the paramedics helped her into the back of the ambulance. Colt stayed behind.

"No," she said. "I need you to come with me."

"There might not be room."

"There's room," the blue-shirted paramedic said. He was busy starting an IV. "You'll need to sit over there, though." He pointed toward the front of the ambulance before poking a needle in Dee's arm.

Dee hated needles.

But he didn't even react to this one. Dear God. He didn't react at all.

She felt nausea building inside her, thought she might lose it then and there. Colt kept her grounded, his big hand holding hers, guiding her toward the padded seat. They would need to put her in a padded *jacket* by the time this was over, she thought morosely.

Dee had had *convulsions.* Why, damn it? *Why?*

"He's going to be all right," she heard Colt say as they started rolling, sirens blaring.

"I don't understand what could have happened."

She raised her voice over the keening wail of the ambulance. "He was fine this morning."

"You're certain this has never happened before?" one of the paramedics asked.

She tore her gaze away from Dee's prone body. "I'm positive."

But she couldn't keep her eyes off Dee for long. He still wore the same white-and-gray-striped shirt as before, his jeans somewhat dusty from his earlier collision with the ground. But in his stillness, he looked like a normal little boy. Except for being hooked up to the IV. The way his tiny body was strapped down…

"No," she said. "Never."

"Well," said one of the ambulance paramedics, his body swaying as they rounded a corner, "he's stable. And his vital signs have returned to normal. Pupils look good. He's just out of it from the seizure. Happens. Well, not necessarily seizures, but I swear the human body goes into some kind of deep sleep after something like this happens. I've seen it a million times." The man smiled reassuringly. "Can I get some information from you?"

Colt watched as Amber nodded, then grabbed a strap hanging by her head as they rounded yet another corner. She answered the paramedic's questions, looking as pale and as drawn as her nephew while they made their way through city streets.

Her nephew.

Colt had known it. Still, such an abrupt confirmation of the fact left him reeling.

He wondered if he should question her. Act surprised, maybe even angry. But in the end, he didn't have it in him.

They arrived at the hospital in minutes. A group of doctors was waiting once the doors opened. From that point forward, things got chaotic. Amber wanted to stay with Dee, but they took the boy into a room and told her to stay out. She didn't like that, but Colt wrapped her in his arms, his chin resting on her head as they waited. And if he wasn't mistaken, Amber cried. Gently and softly.

Dee was her nephew.

Back at Camp Cowboy, Colt had been about to tell her he knew that. Had been right on the verge of confessing everything.

Now wasn't the time.

One of these days he'd have to tell her the truth. The question was would she forgive him?

"Ms. Brooks?" Colt turned to find a nurse standing in the doorway. "The doctors will see you now."

Chapter Seventeen

She hated hospitals. They reminded her of the worst day of her life—the day her sister had died....

"Ms. Brooks," said a Hispanic man with kind brown eyes and a light dusting of gray in his hair. "We'd like to take your nephew down for a CAT scan."

She nodded. "Of course."

"So far, from what we can tell, he suffered a grand mal seizure. He's autistic, isn't he?"

The name tag pinned to his white coat said Dr. Salazar. "He is," she said. She seemed to have lost the ability to project.

"Then I'm sure you know these kinds of seizures aren't unusual for a child with autism."

"He's never had one before."

"I know, and that's reason to be optimistic. This could be something simple. A deficiency in salt, perhaps. Then again, it might be something more serious. It's too early to tell."

She nodded.

He patted her on the back. "There's a waiting

room down the hall. Why don't you and your husband stay there? I'll have someone come get you just as soon as we know anything more."

He's not my husband.

"Thanks," was all she managed to say.

Colt guided her to the waiting room then, his big hands so warm. He was such a comfort to her. She didn't know what she would have done without him. She'd never felt such a keen sense of loneliness.

"It'll be okay," he said softly.

"Will it?"

Nothing in her life was okay. She'd lost her parents when she was five. Her sister had died fifteen years later. She'd had to bury everyone who ever meant anything to her, except Dee. And now Dee was in the hospital....

"I promise you. It'll all be fine."

He'd sat next to her, tipped his hat back, then pulled her into his arms. How long he held her in silence, she didn't know. She sank against him willingly, and slowly allowed her stress to bleed into him.

"My parents and my sister died in a car accident," he said at last.

She gasped, leaning back. "How old were you?"

"Seventeen."

All she could do was shake her head. "I hardly knew mine," she whispered. "They died when my sister and I were really young."

"Yeah, but you didn't think you'd killed them."

She lifted her head. "What?"

She heard him swallow, watched his Adam's apple bob up and down. "I'd told my dad I could handle it."

"Handle what?"

"Changing the brakes. I'd been in auto shop since my freshman year. Rotors were simple. But…" His eyes had gone as dark as obsidian. "I blew it."

She clutched his arm.

"They never officially blamed me." He swallowed again. "But I knew."

"Oh, Colt. You don't really think—"

"Yeah," he said. "I do. I went to the accident scene. Saw the scars on the pavement. One of the tires came off. I must not have tightened the lug nuts all the way. And my family…"

He didn't finish the sentence. He didn't need to.

"But the police. They never said…"

"I was seventeen. About to graduate high school. I suspect they knew, too. They just didn't tell anyone. And why would they? From where they stood it was an accident. I've mulled this over long and hard. In the end I think they figured, why ruin my life? So they never said anything."

She couldn't imagine… No, that wasn't true. Actually, she *could* put herself in his shoes. She'd heard about her sister's accident from a cop at the door. She wondered what she would have done if they'd told her she'd been responsible for her death.

Like Logan.

She straightened suddenly, struck by how all this

must have affected Dee's dad. Had she thought to ask him? Had she even cared?

She felt ashamed.

"What did you do?" she asked.

"Graduated high school. Managed to qualify for the high school rodeo finals, don't ask me how. One of my teachers took pity on me, encouraged me to go to college."

"Did you go?"

"I didn't want to, but, hell, it was a free ride, so I went."

A cowboy with a college degree. Who would have figured? "How old are you?"

"Thirty. You?"

"Twenty-nine."

"We're almost twins," he said with a small smile.

"You compete in rodeos," she said slowly.

He smirked. "You make it sound like I sell drugs."

With Logan as her single example of a rodeo performer was it any wonder? "I just wouldn't have figured a rodeo cowboy as the college type."

"I did what I had to do."

So he could make it through. She read the unspoken truth in his eyes.

"I'm sorry," she said gently.

"No," he said. "*I'm* sorry."

"What do you have to be sorry about?"

But he never had time to answer. "Ms. Brooks?"

"Yes?" She looked up.

Dr. Salazar smiled from the doorway. "CAT scan

looks good. Potassium levels were so low we're treating him for dehydration. He's awake now if you want to see him."

"Yes, of course." She dived out of Colt's arms. "But, wait, you're telling me he's okay," she said as she and Colt followed him out of the room.

"I think so," the doctor said. "We'll need to keep him overnight to get him rehydrated. There's a facility across the way. Rainbow House. It's a place for families to stay during times like these. You'd be right across the street."

Good Lord, she hadn't even thought that far ahead.

"All right."

"I'll make the arrangements," Dr. Salazar offered.

And then they were in Dee's room, and Amber spotted him in the bed, awake and staring into his corner of the room. He seemed bewildered.

"Hey," she said softly.

"We're going to continue running tests," the doctor murmured. "But I'm leaning toward dehydration. Kids like these…"

He didn't finish. She knew the difficulty of caring for an autistic child.

"Is it possible to bring a dog in here?" Colt asked the doctor.

"No," Dr. Salazar said. "No dogs. I'm sorry."

Colt bent toward her and whispered in her ear, "Maybe we can sneak Mac in here by putting him in a bag."

Dee turned his head, looked up at Colt. "Dog."

What weight remained on her shoulders melted away. "Yes, dog." Amber took a seat next to the bed.

"That's a good sign," Dr. Salazar said. "He's re-membering words."

Two weeks ago he'd never even used the word, and yet here he was, associating Colt with Mac. With time, perhaps Mac could help Dee's ability to focus. Perhaps Dee might learn even more words.

She reached out and blindly grabbed Colt's hand. Yes, Dee was in the hospital, but she had someone by her side to help her through it, and that meant so much to her. So very, *very* much.

"I'll go get the paperwork for the Rainbow House."

They stayed until midnight, when the nurse kicked them out and told them to get some rest. Dr. Salazar had given them everything they needed to use one of the rooms across the street. Amber didn't think anybody would be there to greet them, but she was wrong. The place was like a hotel, one staffed by volunteers. They were shown to a space that was more like an apartment.

"If you or your husband need anything, just let me know," said a perky brunette with thick, straight hair. "You can come and go as you like for as long as you need."

She started to correct her, but she was already gone.

"So, if I decide not to stay here with you, does that mean we're getting a divorce?" Colt asked.

Amber smiled, even laughed a little. "Don't be ridiculous."

But when she met his gaze, she saw something in them that made her catch her breath.

"I don't think I should stay, Amber. I really don't."

He was afraid…afraid of what might happen between them. But she wasn't. Not in the least. And even though ten minutes ago she would have sworn all she wanted was a pillow and a bed, now she found herself taking Colt's hand.

"Don't leave," she said, closing the distance between them. "Not yet."

"Amber—"

She wrapped her arms around his neck and pulled his head down. He was so much taller, making her feel feminine and small. She just loved that.

"I need you, Colt Sheridan."

She kissed him. He didn't move. She nuzzled his lips. He still didn't move. She ran her tongue across his mouth slowly.

"Damn you," he muttered, and pulled her to him.
Yes.

His lips had softened, but his body had done the opposite. She could feel the hard length of him nestled against her belly. Every sinewy ridge of his body was pressed up against her. And his mouth… his mouth was so very soft.

"I want to taste you," she said, not caring that she sounded brazen. She licked him again.

He jerked her against him even harder and gasped, "Amber. Jeez. You're killing me."

"I want you," she moaned.

And he wanted her, too, she could tell. His eyes were no longer obsidian, but more like warm amber....

She ran her hand up the front of his pants. He gasped again.

"I don't have any protection," he muttered between clenched teeth.

Well, she supposed that was better than him carrying around something 24/7. "That's okay," she said. "We can make it work."

When he scooped her up in his arms, she knew how this would end, and that was fine with her.

He found the bed, set her on a thick, brown comforter. But he didn't follow her down. She had to grab his hand, had to tug him toward her.

"Come here, cowboy."

Chapter Eighteen

This was madness.

Colt should walk away from the bed. At the very least he should tell her the truth about why he'd really come to Camp Cowboy. "If you still want me after I—"

She slipped her hand beneath the waistband of his jeans and cupped him, "You're going to kill me," he groaned. "I haven't been honest—"

"Honesty later," she said softly. "Unless it really is life and death."

She reached up with her free hand and knocked his hat off. He didn't care. If she wanted to feel him inside her, he was beyond resisting. Honesty could wait.

"Take your clothes off," he commanded.

He saw her eyes flare, saw the way they narrowed not with anger, but with passion. She drew away, then pulled the shirt she'd been wearing off in one quick jerk. She never hesitated, and suddenly he couldn't get undressed fast enough, given how her strip show was causing his body to harden.

She reached behind her, unclasped her bra. Her breasts sprang free, begging for a man's touch. Colt dropped the shirt he didn't even know he'd been holding.

She leaned back and undid the clasp of her jeans. He did the same. She slid the denim down her legs, slowly, erotically. He mimicked her actions, although he had to kick off his boots first. She'd lost her footwear somewhere, but he didn't have time to wonder where or how, because she'd hooked her thumbs on the sides of her sensible undies. No frilly g-strings for her. Watching her strip them off was just as much a tease as if they'd been lace.

"You're so beautiful," he said, sinking down next to her.

The most beautiful woman he'd ever seen, with her curly blond hair splayed around her head, her full breasts.... Her hips were tiny compared to the rest of her, and below those hips was an area he wanted to explore, was dying to taste.

"Come here, Colt," she said again.

What did this beautiful, compassionate creature with a heart as big as an ocean see in him?

He'd lied to her.

He didn't want to think about that now. All he wanted was Amber.

He stepped out of his own underwear. Sank down next to her and once again felt her naked body against his own.

"Colt?"

He reached up and captured her left breast.

"Colt," she repeated, this time with a sigh.

His hand dropped, and she lay there compliantly, even parted for him, as he slid his fingers toward her core.

"Colt," she whispered again, her eyes closing, her head tipping back as he swirled his tongue around her nipple, at the same time touching her intimately. He wanted to see her climax again. Wanted to hear her cries. Had never forgotten what it felt like to bring her pleasure.

But he wanted…

That was just it. He wanted, too. Wanted her. Shook from the effort it took not to cover her body with his own.

His tongue drifted in lazy circles before his teeth lightly nipped her nipple. Her back arched off the bed, and he trailed kisses downward.

"No," she said, clutching at his arms, trying to draw him back up.

He resisted, because he wanted to give her something first. Something she would remember even if she couldn't ever forgive him.

Please, God, let her forgive him.

He tasted her.

She moaned, her hips rising off the bed.

He suckled her.

She cried out in pleasure.

He flicked his tongue against her core.

"Colt." She groaned. "Oh, jeez, Colt."

He could feel her trembling, loved the way her movements became more frenetic, drew pleasure from her soft moans.

"Let go," he urged.

In the next moment she was crying out, her pleasure so sweet that he felt his own body spasm in response. Damn. What was it about her? Why did he feel the need to do it again, to stay there and make her cry out a second time, or a third, or a fourth?

"Now."

"Now?" he asked. Now *what?*

And since he needed instruction, she pulled him toward her, his body sliding up her own.

"Now," she said again, her eyes intense.

He had no protection. Neither did she, he suspected, but he covered her with his body just the same.

And yet he couldn't stop himself.

His knees nudged hers apart, and she was so soft and wet and warm beneath him that he had to grip the pillow near her head to keep himself from thrusting into her.

"Colt," she admonished as he lay poised at her entrance.

Slow, he told himself. *Enjoy it. Savor the moment.*

Because it might not happen again.

There was only right now, this instant, this one incredible moment when he became one with the most incredible woman he'd ever met.

I love you.

He froze.

"Goddamn it," he murmured.

She lifted her hips, wresting control away from him. The second he connected with her warm embrace, there was nothing he could do. He moved into her, closed his eyes, rested his head against the crook of her neck.

He loved her, he realized, pushing into her.

"Colt," she murmured.

He kissed her neck, drew out, slid in again.

He loved her.

He began to move faster. She welcomed every thrust.

He loved her.

Tears rose to his eyes as, for the first time, he understood what it meant to make love to a woman. This wasn't just sex, he thought, kissing her neck, memorizing the taste of her. This was as different from sex as the sun was from the moon. She *was* sunlight. He basked in her warmth, absorbed her heat and energy, all the while thrusting and thrusting and thrusting....

"Colt!" she cried.

And this time he climaxed with her. This time he was the one who moaned in pleasure. He found her lips as he slowly, inexorably, became aware.

A door closed somewhere. The alarm clock next to the bed flashed 12:00 a.m. The room smelled of cinnamon. Or was that Amber?

"I don't think I can move," she said in amusement.

"I don't want to move." He sighed.

She clasped his head with her hands, forced him to look at her. "I don't want you to, either." By the light of the clock, he saw what he least expected.

Tears.

"Amber..."

She was falling for him. She might not love him yet, but it was there, right beneath the surface. He could see it.

And he'd lied to her.

THEY HARDLY SLEPT, but that was okay with Amber. She marveled at how quickly and...diversely he could bring her to pleasure.

In the early hours of the morning she finally drifted off to sleep, only to be woken by the shrill sound of her cell phone.

Dee.

She scrambled to find her pants, as Colt slept soundly beside her.

"Hello?" she said, heart pounding.

"So you *are* going to answer." She didn't recognize the voice.

"Excuse me?"

"Don't tell me you didn't recognize the number."

Her blood ran cold. "Logan," she said quietly.

"When were you going to tell me my son was in the hospital?"

"How did you find out?"

"I called the school to check in with you. Your boss told me."

Damn it. "He shouldn't have told you," she hissed. "I wanted to wait until the doctor was sure Dee was okay before I called. No point in upsetting you unnecessarily."

"That's not your decision to make. I'm his dad."

"*I've* got custody of Dee."

"You won't for long," he said grimly. "Or didn't you wonder why there've been no annoying beeps so far? No message that you're getting a call from an inmate?"

She hadn't thought about it. "Where are you?" she asked, her blood turning cold.

"All that matters is that soon I'll be San Francisco."

Oh, dear God, he was out. They'd set him free.

"How?"

"Early parole."

She clutched the phone.

"He's my son, Amber."

"And he's *my* nephew," she said. "And you should have thought about the consequences of your actions the night you… The day you…"

She couldn't finish the sentence, and damn it all to hell, she was on the verge of tears. She'd worried about this for so long, had thought there was no way he'd ever get out of jail before his six years were up. She should have known better.

"I *have* thought about it," he said. And much to

her surprise, he sounded almost sad. "Every frickin' day of my life I've thought about it."

"It was a choice," she said. "One that cost my sister her life." *And custody of your son.*

"We had decided to get back together again," he stated. "I've told you before, we were celebrating."

"Yeah, right," she scoffed.

"I know you don't believe me," he said, and for a second she heard something in his voice, something she'd never heard before. Sorrow. Pain. Guilt. "You've never believed me, but I'm telling you the truth, Amber. Just like I'm telling you the God's honest truth now. I want my son back."

"We'll be gone."

"You told me you'd let me see him."

"That was before."

"Before you knew you'd be seeing me face-to-face? Without Plexiglas between us?"

"Something like that," she murmured.

"I knew you hadn't changed. He told me you had. That you weren't as horrible as I thought, but you are."

"Who told you I'd changed?"

"The friend who's done me a favor. He actually begged me to give you a chance. It's why I'm calling. Because I wanted to believe him."

She didn't think it was possible for her blood to turn colder, but it did. "Who?" she asked.

"Doesn't matter."

But she knew. She just *knew*.

"I swear to you, Logan, if you really want me to bring Dee to you, you'll tell me who it is."

"Dee? Is that what you call him?"

"It's what I've always called him."

"No wonder why he didn't put two and two together."

"Who?"

There was a momentary pause. "Colt Sheridan. Sound familiar?"

She squeezed her eyes closed. Clenched the cell phone. "Oh, yeah. It sounds familiar all right."

"I offered to give him one of my old rope horses in exchange for his help."

"Really?" she said. "What a deal."

And then she turned off the phone.

Chapter Nineteen

"You *son* of a *bitch!*"

Colt's eyes snapped open, the room still dark though it was early morning.

"You lying sack of—"

He sat up in bed, shocked to see Amber standing over him, a look in her eyes unlike any he'd ever seen on a woman's face before.

"Get out," she snarled.

"What?" he asked, blinking the sleep from his eyes. "Amber, what's going on?"

"I can't believe you," she said. "You traded us off for a rope horse."

"Rope horse? What are you—" His spine snapped upright. *Holy...*

She knew.

"Amber, calm down."

"Calm down? You want me to *calm down?*"

Her usually pale skin was flushed red. "Get out," she repeated, pointing toward the door. But then she seemed to crumple. She lifted her hands to her mouth, tears pouring from her eyes. "Get out, you son of a bitch," she sobbed. "Now."

He pulled the covers off and went to her. "No. I'm not leaving. Not until I explain."

"Explain what?" She stepped away from him before he could touch her. "That you were spying on me. That two weeks you were at Camp Cowboy to report back to Logan. Logan!" she said, her mouth trembling. "The one man on earth I loathe." She hissed in a breath.

Colt tried to calm *himself* down, but there was no escaping the bitter truth. He'd done exactly as she accused.

"I didn't mean to hurt you," he said. "I…" God, he didn't know what to say. "When I started working at Camp Cowboy, I expected to meet a selfish, arrogant woman. That's how Logan made you sound. Instead I met you."

"And that's supposed to make me feel better?" she asked. "Well, it doesn't."

She had no reason to forgive him. "Yes, I got the job at Camp Cowboy as a way of getting close to you."

She wiped her eyes, and it broke his heart.

"As a way to find Dee." He swallowed. "In exchange for a rope horse."

She quietly sobbed.

"And I'm so sorry, Amber. I never meant for things to turn out like this. I never expected to fall in love with you."

She huffed out a laugh. "Love," she said. "Hah."

"I do love you."

"Then why didn't you tell me the truth?"

"I *tried* to," he said. "Just before Dee got sick, when we were in the hallway, I tried."

"Save it," she said, holding up a hand. He wanted to wipe away the tear tracks on her face.

"No," he said. "I'm not going to save it." He tried to touch her. "I love you, Amber. I don't know how it happened. Don't know how it's possible when we practically just met, but I do love you."

"I'm leaving," she said.

He realized then that she was dressed, and that her hair was brushed and her shoes were on.

"No," he said, darting in front of her. "Don't go."

"Get out of my way, Colt."

"Amber, please. Yes, I got hired at Camp Cowboy because of you, but then I started working with the kids. Watched what happened when you worked with them and it…touched me." And goddamn it all to hell, he felt tears come to his own eyes. "The past two weeks have meant more to me than the past many years," he said, reaching out a hand.

She flinched away from his touch.

"Yes, I was in contact with Logan, but it was to ask him not to take Dee away from you. And I didn't tell him where Dee was. I swear to you."

She'd stopped crying. From somewhere deep inside her she'd found strength. God, he wished he could, too. "I don't believe you." She stepped around him.

"Amber—"

But she was gone.

"Damn it!" Colt slammed his fist against the wall, only to collapse to the floor a moment later and cry... cry as he hadn't done since the day his family died.

SHE WENT BACK to the hospital, but not before alerting security that she had a stalker who had tracked her to the facility. It was the truth, or close enough to the truth that it must have shown in her eyes. She didn't want to see Colt, either, so she told them nobody was allowed inside. The black-clothed security guard didn't hesitate. "I'll get right on it."

Whatever the officer did, it must have worked. She didn't see Colt. She went back to Dee's room and pasted a bright smile on her face.

"Everything looks good," Dr. Salazar reported an hour later. "He was dehydrated. Probably the new environment. You know how kids like this are. They'll spit stuff out when you're not looking. You might want to monitor his fluids for the next week or two. I'll send instructions along to the home he's in."

"Thanks," she said softly.

Dr. Salazar cocked his head. "You okay? You look worried."

"No, no," she said. "I'm fine. Just tired." She forced another smile. "Long night."

"I'm sure it was. But things will get better from here on out. You can take him back to this residence—" he glanced down at his paperwork "—Camp Cowboy."

"Thanks," she said.

"Good luck, Ms. Brooks. It's not easy dealing with a child like Dee. Get some rest. You look like you need it."

"Yeah," she huffed, holding back tears. "I think you're right."

He patted her on the arm and left the room. Amber sat in the chair to wait for the discharge papers. Dee sat in his bed, staring at the TV above it as if it held answers to all the questions in the universe…and maybe it did.

"Here we go," a nurse said eventually, startling her. "All ready." She was pushing a wheelchair, their discharge papers on the seat. "Will your nephew listen to instructions?"

"Not really," Amber said, getting up. "But it's always worth a try."

She sat on the edge of Dee's bed. "Dee, we're leaving."

No reaction.

She dipped her head in front of him, blocked his vision. "You ready to go, kiddo?"

He leaned away from her, eyes so much like her sister's staring upward.

I want to see my son.

And he'd sounded so sincere. Almost desperate. She'd never heard Logan talk like that.

"Come on," she said, slowly reaching for Dee's hand. He jerked when she touched him.

It was one thing too many.

"Please, Dee," she said. "Don't make this hard on me. I don't think I can take it today."

He didn't move.

"I love you, kiddo," she said, trying to keep from crying…again. Damn it. She couldn't lose him. Couldn't bear not being a part of his life. "Auntie loves you so much." She needed to hold on to that thought. That was all that mattered.

She stood, held out her hand.

"Come on."

Dee actually listened.

Gil had sent a car earlier that afternoon. It was a short ride back to Camp Cowboy, but it took every ounce of her resolve to get out when they arrived. What if she saw Colt? What would she do? What should she do? Should she tell Gil what he'd done?

But, as it turned out, she needn't have worried.

"Did you hear what happened?" Melissa asked. "Colt quit. Just up and packed his bags and left. Buck and Gil are beside themselves."

"I'm not surprised," Amber heard herself answer, though she wasn't certain if she was responding to Melissa's comments about Buck and Gil or the fact that Colt had quit. "I'm going to settle Dee into his room."

"You need any help?" Melissa called.

But they were halfway up the stairs. "No," she said. "I'll be fine."

But she wasn't fine. From the moment she'd first caught sight of the lodge, she thought she might be sick. Didn't think she would have the strength to climb the steps. Dee had darted ahead of her, obviously remembering the way to his room. By the time she caught up to him in the doorway, he was standing in his corner again, only this time facing out.

"Dog?" he asked, his head turning this way and that.

Amber caught her breath.

He turned around. "Dog?"

She lifted a hand to her mouth, tried to fight back even more damn tears. "No, Dee," she said softly. "No dog."

Her nephew continued to search his room. "Maaac," he called. "Mac!"

A sob broke free. "Oh, Dee."

"Mac!"

"He's gone, Dee. They're both gone."

And then she was on the floor, without knowing how she'd got there. She couldn't stop herself from crying. She didn't want to lose Dee. Didn't want to lose Colt.

"He's gone," she repeated.

"I love you, kiddo."

Amber looked up. Her mouth dropped open. Dee stood above her, his hand outstretched.

"Dee love you," he said, his brown eyes full of compassion.

Chapter Twenty

She wouldn't take his calls. Colt didn't blame her. If he'd been in her shoes he wouldn't have taken his calls, either.

He did something he hadn't done in a long time then. Something he never thought he'd do. He went back to his family's ranch in Texas. The place where he'd grown up.

The northern part of the state wasn't the dry desert everyone thought it was. There were areas of green. Valleys and canyons with landlocked lakes. It was beautiful country. Perfect for raising cattle.

He turned down the narrow, two-lane road that led to his parents' home. That's what it was—his parents' place. It had never been his. The two-story ranch house was deserted, as he'd known it would be.

Except for the extreme dust and spiderwebs, it was exactly as he'd left it.

Ten years ago he'd packed up and headed out on the rodeo trail. Occasionally he would come back, when a competition brought him nearby, but for the most part he'd stayed away. It was too painful to return. So he'd lived the life of a hobo, staying this place and that.

He tried calling her one last time, and when that failed, broke down and phoned Logan.

"So you finally decided to call me back?" his old friend asked, but he didn't sound angry.

"Had a hell of a time tracking you down," Colt admitted, sitting in one of his mother's kitchen chairs. They were old, with hollow aluminum legs and vinyl seats. Buttercup-yellow. The whole kitchen was yellow. He didn't have the heart to change it… not yet. "Last time we talked, you didn't have a cell phone."

"How'd you find me?" Logan asked.

"Rodeo crowd." Colt absently patted Mac's head.

"Ahh," Logan said. "Word of mouth."

Colt swallowed. "Have you seen her?"

There was a pause. "Next week, as a matter of fact," he said. "Amazingly, she actually called me and set up a time."

"So you're going to take him back?"

There was another pause. "I don't know what I'm going to do just yet."

And in the words Colt heard sorrow…and regret.

"Why'd you make her out to be a witch?" Colt asked.

"She was," Logan said. Colt pictured his friend. Dark hair. Dark eyes. So very like Dee. It was remarkable that Dee had so much of both parents in him. Yet again, Colt was shocked he hadn't put two and two together far sooner than he had. "Or she has been."

"She isn't now?" Colt asked, getting up and staring out the kitchen window. Rolling hills stretched as far as the eye could see.

A thousand acres.

It had been a bitch to keep current on the property taxes, but he had. The whole place was his. No mortgage. No liens. Just land. His father's land, and his father's father's before that.

"She's…different now," Logan said. "More willing to talk to me about Rudy."

Rudy. The name Logan would always call his son. Just like Amber would always call the boy Dee. Her pet name.

"How is he?" Colt asked, clutching the counter in front of him.

"Good. No more seizures. She's thinking it really was diet related."

"I hear that can happen with autistic children."

Another pause. "Yeah, I guess he really *is* autistic, isn't he? But Amber's staying on top of things now."

As she always had.

"Hey, listen," Colt said. "If you see her, will you give her a message?"

"I don't know," Logan said. "I have a feeling mentioning your name to Amber might ruin our new-found friendship."

But Colt could tell his friend was joking. Whatever had happened to him all those years ago, whatever had caused the drinking, the partying, the carousing, it was over now. Colt had no doubt Logan was ready to take on the duties of fatherhood.

"Tell her I'm sorry," he said. "And that I wish…I wish things could have been different."

"I'll do that," Logan promised. "You coming out to California again anytime soon?"

"No," Colt said. "I'm done with rodeo."

"You sure? I still got my old rope horse out in Morgan's pasture."

"No." Colt glanced out the window once more. "I'm going to try and make a go of it here."

Logan paused again. "Good for you."

"And good for you, too. Tell Dee that Mac says hello."

And that I miss him.

Miss them both.

SHE'D BEEN DREADING the meeting for weeks. But a deal was a deal, Amber thought. She'd promised Logan she'd give him a chance. That he could spend some time with Dee…if for no other reason than to convince him that keeping Dee in an institution was the right thing to do.

She'd chosen a neutral spot—Golden Gate Park, just a little distance from Camp Cowboy. It had dawned a beautiful day. The fog that had plagued the camp for weeks had disappeared. So they'd spent the morning walking to Baker Beach. It had been a bit of a hike, but Amber didn't care. It was so green and peaceful. The peninsula was on a slope, and she could see breakers rolling toward shore. The Golden Gate Bridge was off in the distance, its shadow seeming to undulate on the choppy sea. Dee hung back, his eyes firmly on the crashing waves.

Rudy. Dee.

That's why Colt hadn't put two and two together. Logan had confessed it all. How he'd sent Colt to find Dee, since she wouldn't tell him where Dee was. How Colt had begged him not to do it.

Colt hadn't been lying about that. She didn't know what to think.

"Hello, Amber."

She stiffened. She'd been expecting the meeting. She should be nice. This was, after all, Dee's father.

"Logan," she said, turning to face him.

He'd aged.

It shocked her, this first glimpse of him. His black hair had gone gray around the edges, though he was barely in his thirties. Usually a little on the long side, it was close-cropped. His eyes were still the same warm brown, but they held the weight of the world.

"I didn't think you'd come."

She shrugged, returned to staring at the ocean. Sailboats were zigzagging through the channel. "We made a deal."

"Rudy?" Logan said gently, far more gently than Amber would have ever thought possible from him.

"He likes the waves," she found herself saying,

even though the last thing she'd told herself to do was try to soften this meeting. Dee's autism was why Logan had left in the first place. Why her sister had called it quits all those years ago. He couldn't take living with an autistic child.

"Rudy?" he said again, stepping in front of him.

Amber was stunned. The old Logan would have made some ridiculous comment. Would have claimed, "I can fix him." Would have argued with her when she explained that Dee's condition couldn't be fixed.

This Logan squatted near Dee. "Hey, son." He didn't clutch his shoulder. Didn't force him to turn and look at him.

"It's me, Rudy…Dee," Logan corrected. "Dad." Amber watched as he swallowed. "I'm your dad."

Dee didn't look at him. Didn't even move. Just stared out at the ocean.

And Amber could see the hurt in Logan's eyes.

"It's nothing personal," she said. "He's like that with everyone, even me. But he's aware. I swear to you, Logan, he knows everything you say."

That had been illustrated to her perfectly on that day she'd been sobbing in the child's room.

Dee loves you.

Logan glanced up at her, his hair blowing in the breeze off the ocean. "Are you sure?"

"Positive."

Dee's father stood back up. And Amber noticed he was even dressing differently. No jeans this time out. He wore brown slacks. And a dark-brown, button down shirt instead of a T-shirt. But most impressive was that he didn't try to touch his son. Didn't try to hug him. Didn't do anything the old Logan would have done.

"Give it time," Amber said.

Logan nodded, then turned so he could follow where his son was looking. They stood there together for goodness knows how long. Amber was so completely transfixed by the sight. She'd always thought Dee looked like her sister. But that wasn't true.

Dee resembled his dad.

She swallowed hard. How she not seen that before?

She hadn't wanted to.

But this wasn't the man she remembered.

"He never told me where he was, you know," Logan said.

"Pardon?"

"Colt," Logan said. "He didn't betray you like you think he did. He'd already put it together, who Dee was. A week before Dee got sick, he knew. But he never told me where Dee was specifically. Instead, he begged me to give it a chance. To trust you. I have the email if you want to see it."

"No."

Logan came over and placed a hand on her shoulder.

Amber wanted to cry.

"He told me I owe you big time." He half turned.

"For everything you've done. And I know I do, Amber. I really do." He looked down at the sand. "I messed up." And there were tears in his eyes. "I really messed up." The wind caught his hair again. "But I'm sorry. For everything, Amber. I'm so damn sorry, and I *swear* to you I'll make it up." She heard his voice hitch. "I don't know if I ever can. But I swear I'm going to try."

She couldn't breathe for a moment. How had this happened? How had a man who'd been so horrible, changed so much?

She couldn't deny that he had.

Sharron would have wanted her to move forward.

"You don't need to make it up to me."

"Yes, I do," he said. "I do. And I promise I'll be there for the both of you. I swear to you, Amber."

They both glanced at Dee. The little boy had turned. A second later he lifted his hand and pointed. "Mac!"

It was like a stab to the heart. "No, Dee, that's not—"

But it was.

A dog that looked just like Mac ran forward, a gray-and-white speeding bullet that hurled itself straight at Dee.

"This is step one of making it up to you," Logan said. "He loves you, Amber. I've never met a man so devoted to a woman. Your rejection is killing him. Please, give him a chance."

Because beyond Mac, walking along the edge of

the beach toward her, was Colt, black cowboy hat firmly in place.

"Oh, damn," she muttered.

Through eyes suddenly filled with tears, she watched as Mac threw himself at Dee's feet.

"Mac!" Dee cried.

That was all the incentive the dog needed. Rear end swaying, tongue lolling, eyes wide and bright, Mac rubbed up against the little boy he loved so much.

"Mac," Dee repeated, squatting and burying his head in the dog's thick fur.

She had to look away. If she didn't she'd start bawling like a baby.

"Hello, Amber."

She still found herself dashing tears away, having to inhale deeply before facing him. She should be angry. She should tell both of them, Logan and Colt, to get lost.

"I hope you're not mad at Logan," Colt said.

The sound of the ocean was nothing compared to the roar in her ears. "I'm not," she said, uncertain what she felt. But it wasn't anger.

Colt blocked her view, so she had to look at him.

"I went back to Texas, Amber," he said. "I went back and faced my inner demons."

She inhaled deeply. "And?" Something inside her shifted as she looked into his blue eyes.

"All alone, surrounded by a thousand acres...all I wanted was you," he said, reaching out to brush a lock of her hair away from her eyes. "And I found I couldn't live without you."

"Colt…"

"I hated myself before I met you, Amber. I couldn't see the good in anything…or in anybody. And then you came along."

She tried again. "Colt…"

"And I realized that if a woman like you could like a man like me…"

She shook her head.

"That if someone who only saw the good in things could find some good in me… And if she wasn't afraid to put everything on the line, then I could do no less."

Her vision began to blur. He reached for her hands.

"I love you, Amber. I love you more than I've loved anything in my life."

Except his parents and his sister. But he didn't need to qualify it. His family that he'd loved so much, and that he blamed himself for killing. But he'd forgiven himself now. Amber had taught him how to do that. She'd forgiven the man who'd killed her sister. How could he do less? She could see it in his eyes.

"I love you," he repeated earnestly, cupping her face in his hands.

She loved him, too. Still. With him standing in front of her, there was no way she could deny it.

"You lied to me," she whispered.

"I might not have been honest about my reasons for coming to Camp Cowboy, but I never lied."

"But it was dishonest."

"Yes," he admitted, "it was. And I'm sorry. I'm so damn sorry."

He clutched her hands again. "I love you," he repeated. "Please tell me you forgive me."

She drew a deep breath, inhaled the scent of him and absorbed the feel of his body.

"Marry me?" he asked.

She looked past him, at Logan, who'd been kind enough to step away and give them some privacy. At Dee, who sat stroking Colt's dog. And at the sky, so blue and beautiful and so much like Colt's eyes.

"Marry me?" He tipped her chin up and forced her to look at him.

He loved her.

"Marry me."

He kissed her. And the moment their lips touched, she knew it was useless. She loved this man. He might have met her under false pretenses, might not have been exactly honest, but she loved him. And when he kissed her, she couldn't doubt that he loved her right back.

"Marry me," he said a fourth time.

And this time when she looked him in the eyes she answered, "Yes."

He jerked her to him so quickly and so suddenly that she gasped. And then she was laughing. And crying. And hugging him back.

"Dee love Mac."

They both glanced over in time to see Dee plop down on the beach as he wrapped his arm around Colt's dog.

"Good dog," the little boy said.

And then they were both smiling and laughing, as for the first time, Amber felt hope. Colt loved her. Dee loved Colt's dog. Amber loved Colt. And if Dee continued to speak, that was a minor miracle in and of itself.

The *second* miracle of her life.

* * * * *

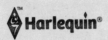

Harlequin®

COMING NEXT MONTH

Available November 8, 2011

#1377 A TEXAS RANGER'S CHRISTMAS
American Romance's Men of the West
Rebecca Winters

#1378 HOLIDAY IN A STETSON
Marie Ferrarella and Tina Leonard

#1379 MY CHRISTMAS COWBOY
Men of Red River
Shelley Galloway

#1380 THE CHRISTMAS SECRET
Fatherhood
Lee McKenzie

HARCNM1011

REQUEST YOUR FREE BOOKS!
2 FREE NOVELS PLUS 2 FREE GIFTS!

LOVE, HOME & HAPPINESS

Harlequin® Special Edition® is thrilled to present a new installment in USA TODAY bestselling author RaeAnne Thayne's reader-favorite miniseries, THE COWBOYS OF COLD CREEK.

Join the excitement as we meet the Bowmans—four siblings who lost their parents but keep family ties alive in Pine Gulch. First up is Trace. Only two things get under this rugged lawman's skin: beautiful women and secrets. And in Rebecca Parsons, he finds both!

Read on for a sneak peek of CHRISTMAS IN COLD CREEK. *Available November 2011 from Harlequin® Special Edition®.*

On impulse, he unfolded himself from the bar stool. "Need a hand?"

"Thank you! I…" She lifted her gaze from the floor to his jeans and then raised her eyes. When she identified him her hazel eyes turned from grateful to unfriendly and cold, as if he'd somehow thrown the broken glasses at her head.

He also thought he saw a glimmer of panic in those interesting depths, which instantly stirred his curiosity like cream swirling through coffee.

"I've got it, Officer. Thank you." Her voice was several degrees colder than the whirl of sleet outside the windows.

Despite her protests, he knelt down beside her and began to pick up shards of broken glass. "No problem. Those trays can be slippery."

This close, he picked up the scent of her, something fresh and flowery that made him think of a mountain meadow on a July afternoon. She had a soft, lush mouth and for one brief, insane moment, he wanted to push aside that stray lock of hair slipping from her ponytail and taste her. Apparently he needed to spend a lot less time working and a great deal *more* time recreating with the opposite sex if he could have sudden random fantasies about a woman he wasn't even inclined to like, pretty or not.

"I'm Trace Bowman. You must be new in town."

She didn't answer immediately and he could almost see the wheels turning in her head. Why the hesitancy? And why that little hint of unease he could see clouding the edge of her gaze? His presence was obviously making her uncomfortable and Trace couldn't help wondering why.

"Yes. We've been here a few weeks."

"Well, I'm just up the road about four lots, in the white house with the cedar shake roof, if you or your daughter need anything." He smiled at her as he picked up the last shard of glass and set it on her tray.

Definitely a story there, he thought as she hurried away. He just might need to dig a little into her background to find out why someone with fine clothes and nice jewelry, and who so obviously didn't have experience as a waitress, would be here slinging hash at The Gulch. Was she running away from someone? A bad marriage?

So...Rebecca Parsons. Not Becky. An intriguing woman. It had been a long time since one of those had crossed his path here in Pine Gulch.

Trace won't rest until he finds out Rebecca's secret, but will he still have that same attraction to her once he does? Find out in CHRISTMAS IN COLD CREEK. Available November 2011 from Harlequin® Special Edition®.

HSEEXPI111

Harlequin *Super Romance*

Discover a fresh, heartfelt new romance
from acclaimed author

Sarah Mayberry

Businessman Flynn Randall's life is
complicated. So he doesn't need the
distraction of fun, spontaneous Mel Porter.
But he can't stop thinking about her. Maybe
he can handle one more complication....

All They Need

LONGER BOOK
Same Price!

*Available November 8, 2011,
wherever books are sold!*

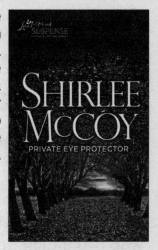

Discover two classic tales of romance in one
incredible volume from

USA TODAY **Bestselling Author**

Catherine Mann

Two powerful, passionate men
are determined to win back the women
who haunt their dreams...but it will
take more than just seduction
to convince them that this love will last.

IRRESISTIBLY HIS

Available October 25, 2011.